PARALLELS

JAMES KINSLEY

DEIXIS PRESS

Copyright © James Kinsley 2025
All rights reserved.

The right of James Kinsley to be identified as the author of this work has been asserted by him in accordance with the Copyright, Designs and Patents Act 1988.

This book is a work of fiction. Names, characters, businesses, and incidents either are products of the author's imagination or are used in a fictitious manner. Any resemblance to actual persons, living or dead, events, or locales is entirely coincidental.

First published in 2025 by Deixis Press
www.deixis.press

ISBN 978-1-917090-06-3 (HB)
ISBN 978-1-917090-07-0 (PB)

Typeset using Science Fair and Avenir Next by
Palimpsest Book Production Ltd, Falkirk, Stirlingshire

Editoral work by Angel Belsey, Ben Henley and Damian Abbott

Cover design by Deividas Jablonskis

PARALLELS

JAMES KINSLEY

For Karen

WOKE UP LOST...

1

Chongqing, late summer. At this time of day, the streets should be bustling, despite the region's ferocious temperature and humidity, with throngs of shoppers and workers. Foreign tourists were rare this far inside mainland China, but domestic tourists would make up a fair proportion of the city's crowds.

Not so this year. The streets were deserted, and it was unfeasibly cold, snow whipped up into miniature twisters by the bitter wind, drifting in the alleyways and side streets. From further down the main thoroughfare that cut through this commercial sector of the megacity, a low rumbling became audible and, a few moments later, a tank hove into view, its tracks grinding into the snow. It pulled to a stop at the point the road opened out into a plaza, outside a department store, mannequins incongruously dressed in the latest summer fashions watching on. Almost simultaneously, two hatches opened: one in the top turret and one lower down, on the main hull. Two heads appeared, one from each.

"This is fucking ridiculous. You're telling me you've no idea where we are?"

Price's voice was thick with disgust. The tank commander pulled himself up into a standing position within the turret. He yanked his headphones off and wrestled a battered pack of cigarettes from the chest pocket of his thick jacket. Lighting one, he snorted out an exasperated plume of blue smoke through his unkempt moustache before turning his attention back to the other head. "So what, we're completely lost?"

Jezz muttered something to himself and disappeared back into the hull briefly. He reappeared clutching a map which, after brushing aside a small amount of snow that had started to settle on the hull, he proceeded to try and smooth down. Price extricated himself from out of the turret, slithering down the outside of the tank to end up next to where Jezz was propped up in his hatch.

Jezz stabbed a finger on the map. "Look, we started here, we've come down here," stabbing his finger again, "so we must be somewhere around here." With the last 'here', he drew his finger around in a circle, a larger circle than Price wanted to see, encompassing a sizeable portion of the district.

"And we've no GPS at all?"

"If we had GPS," sighed Jezz, blowing on his hands and rubbing them together, "I would know where we fucking were, wouldn't I."

Price scowled. "This is fucking ridiculous," he muttered again to himself.

"It's not my fault, Price. GPS is useless this close to the front, you know that. And I'm not trained for… for this paper bullshit," Jezz half-scrunched the map up as he shook it in frustration at Price.

Price could see the logo of the multinational conglomerate they were nominally employees of on the corner of the map. The same logo was on his jacket and, somewhat vulgarly despoiled, on the side of their tank. Jezz was right, it wasn't like any of them were trained for this. They weren't regular Army. Like approximately a third of the fighting forces in Sichuan Province, they were volunteers, part of the emergency deployment put together by patriotic organisations of varying types to supplement the regular armed forces in what was rapidly becoming a fight for humanity's very existence.

It had been nine months since the first Eltiy'ch ships had landed. Nine months since humanity had finally received the answer to the question that had preoccupied it for millennia. They were not alone. First Contact had occurred and, almost instantaneously, they had been plunged into a war that it seemed would either define them or destroy them.

"Well, fuck," said Price, finally. He banged his fist on the hull twice. Jezz pulled himself up out of his hatch, then reached back down inside to retrieve his rifle. From the turret, Nora appeared, rifle at the ready and already taking a sweep of the street as she lowered herself to the ground. The massive, bearded head of the fourth member of the crew emerged behind her, looking for all the world like a Viking beserker. The Finn, Teemu, swore an oath as he looked around. "Where are we?"

"We don't know," snapped Price. "So get out and see if you can work it out."

"What do you mean, work it out? I'm a fucking homing pigeon now?"

"I don't know," said Price, exasperation raw in his voice. "Find a road sign or a shop name, or something."

Teemu shrugged and started to climb up out of the tank.

Jezz was already on the ground by this time, tracking through the snow behind Nora, covering her as she scouted ahead to the next junction. He was just about to call out to her, to warn her about getting too far from the tank, when she froze.

They may have not been regular army, but five months as volunteers in Sichuan Province had given the crew all the instincts of combat veterans. The other three all snapped into a state of high alert, weapons ready. Jezz softly slipped the safety catch off on his rifle, knowing Price and Teemu would be doing exactly the same behind him. Crouching, he scuttled to the side of the street, sheltering in the doorway of the department store, and brought his rifle up, scanning the street ahead for threats. The eerie silence of the immediate area made Jezz nervous. He frantically switched his gaze from shop window to shop window and back to the street, looking for and hoping not to find signs of movement. He focused on calming his breathing.

Nora was now backing slowly towards them, her attention focused further down the road. Jezz couldn't tell if there were dark shapes moving at the far end of the thoroughfare, or whether it was just shadows, his mind playing tricks on him. He looked back at the tank. Teemu was nowhere to be seen, presumably back inside. Price was kneeling down, his back up against the tracks of the tank, offering no outline to any watching Eltiy'ch. Seeing Jezz looking back at him, Price gestured impatiently at him, urging him back towards the tank and (relative) safety.

Nora had now fallen back almost to Jezz's position, so he responded to Price's order and started to make his own way back along the side of the department store, towards the tank. He was about six feet from the vehicle when Nora suddenly opened fire, directing a short burst at some unseen enemy. Price shouted something, before opening fire himself. Nora turned and ran, keeping low, towards the tank.

At first, Jezz couldn't see any targets. His eyes darted in panic from one side of the street to the other. He was reluctant to make a break for the tank until he'd at least identified where the threat was. Then, all of a sudden, his perception of the street seemed to shift. Like a sailboat coalescing from the swirls of a magic eye drawing, dark shapes came into focus out of the shadows. Bringing his rifle to bear on the nearest target, Jezz bared his teeth as he fired off a quick burst of automatic fire. The alien figure pitched forward into the snow.

But Jezz knew that success has a tendency to make you a target. Before the Eltiy'ch's comrades could get a fix on him, he pushed away from the wall of the department store and ran hell-for-leather towards the tank. Price, yelling at Jezz to get a fucking move on, was standing now, switching his focus from one side of the street to the other as he fired short bursts from his rifle, trying to force the advancing scout party into cover to allow his crew the chance to get back to the tank.

The exchange of fire was momentarily drowned out by the deep rumbling growl of the tank's engines coming to life. Price pulled himself up onto the hull and scrambled into the turret hatch, almost pitching into the vehicle headfirst. Jezz pulled himself up onto the front of the hull, making for his own hatch. He turned. "NORA!"

He needn't have worried; she was practically behind him. She was scowling at him, waving at him furiously to get inside and so out of her way, when Jezz saw a Eltiy'ch scout appear just metres away. He started to bring his rifle up, but for a second was distracted by a figure behind the alien. A human figure. Slight, pale, short hair. What the hell were civilians doing out here? He froze, unable to open fire for fear of hitting the woman. Nora was on the hull now, yelling at him frantically. He blinked. The civilian was gone. What the hell?

Nora shoved him violently towards the hatch, ducking to give Price, now stood in the upper hatch, a clear line of fire at the alien troopers in the street. As Jezz fell into the hatch, the last thing he saw before landing roughly in his seat was the Eltiy'ch scout raising one of its arms and throwing something. In desperation, Jezz threw himself out of his seat and towards the box his gas mask was stored in. A small, metal projectile the size of a baseball came through the hatch after him, a dark red smoke already leaking from one end…

2

Jezz awoke, sitting bolt upright, heart racing, thudding in his chest as if it were trying to escape through his ribs. For a moment, he felt the echo of confinement, as if his body had been restrained. He realised he was drenched, the odour of sweat filling his nostrils. Sweat, and something else, something oily. Throwing the covers off, he swung his legs around off the bed, instinctively reaching for the bottle of water on his bedside cabinet…

Jeff paused, hand extended. Not Jezz. Jeff. What was… He shook his head, trying to break the thoughts down, letting the truth separate from the imaginary and settle on the surface. Jeff, thirty-four years old, programmer. Not a soldier. Not in Sichuan province. Not in… Chongjin? Just… what? He looked over to the other side of the bed, to where… No, that wouldn't help. Jeff finished reaching for the bottle, unscrewing the top and taking a long pull on it. He rubbed his chin, the real world re-establishing itself, restoring order. He coughed, once, a phlegmy feeling in his mouth. He grimaced as he swallowed.

He was alone in the double bed, the ongoing nightmare of his relationship breakdown penetrating the remnants of the dreamscape that still whirled in his brain. He remembered with a dull ache that there was no need to worry about waking anyone if he were to turn the lamp on, so he did. Taking another swig of water, he put the bottle back and picked up his watch. Ten past six. The worst of all times to wake up. Early enough before his alarm was due to go off to feel cheated, not early enough to go back to sleep. Jeff cursed and ran his hands through his hair, noting with discomfort that his hair, too, was slick with sweat.

The dream had been vivid, as they so often were since starting on his current medication. It was a weird one though, the war in… he shook his head as the details of his dream already started to slip through his fingers. Sighing, he pushed himself up from the bed and sloped into the bathroom. There may not be aliens to fight out there, but he had a busy day at wo…

He paused as he looked at himself in the bathroom mirror. The tired eyes staring back out at him from his pallid, drawn face reminded him that he didn't have that, either. His boss had been pretty clear about that. Having not taken any leave in eight months, since Ciara had left, Jeff was on an extended break, under strict instructions to get some proper rest. The insinuation clear, that when he returned, he had better be in better shape.

No work, then. Jeff stared at himself for a couple more minutes, before going back to bed. He needn't worry about the alarm, of course. He'd not set it.

Jeff slept a couple more hours, before finally dragging himself back out of bed. He made his way downstairs just before ten. Unplugging his phone, he gave it a quick onceover as the kettle boiled. No need to take too long, the notifications were few. A WhatsApp from Anoush, a text from Anya. A few unexciting Facebook notifications. His email inbox was empty. He put the phone down again and made himself a cup of tea.

He carried the tea and a large bowl of cereal through to his living room, slumping down on his armchair. He flicked on the tv. His brain, still clinging on to the remnants of the dream from the night before, half expected to see something about the war on the news, but there was nothing, obviously. Flicking over from the BBC news channel to something even more depressing, he watched, glassy-eyed, as three female presenters tried to instil in him excitement for some moron's self-inflicted consumer complaint. He barely registered, let alone enjoyed, the cereal he was mechanically spooning into his mouth. Consumer affairs morphed into antiques, antiques segued into property. In no time at all, lunchtime quizzes loomed.

In the end, even Jeff's tolerance for vegetating had limits. Showered and dressed and out of the house by noon, this felt like an achievement. It was more than he'd managed the first few days of his enforced leave. He would be the first to admit, too, that feeling clean, properly clean, especially after awaking in a pool of his own sweat, was a genuinely pleasant sensation. He probably felt as human this morning as he'd felt at any point since starting his leave. If not longer.

He stopped for hot chocolate and a Danish at a small coffee shop on the edge of the town centre. There was a book shop opposite, a small independent one. Jeff sat in the window of the coffee shop watching the foot traffic in front of the book shop. Occasionally, somebody would stop and look at something in the window that had caught their eye, or enter the shop, at which point Jeff would try and guess what sort of book they would be looking for. Alas, none of those that came out were brandishing their purchases in such a way as to allow him to see how right or wrong he'd been, but nevertheless, it was a reasonably diverting way to spend an hour or so. He ordered a second cup of hot chocolate.

A young woman stopped briefly by the book shop window. Very pale, very slender, with a platinum blonde elfin cut, jeans, fashionable jacket, expensive looking trainers. She looked like porcelain. It wasn't difficult to imagine why she had particularly caught Jeff's eye. He considered for a moment... then shook his head. What was he thinking? His skin crawled at the audacity of it.

Instead, he went up to the counter and settled his bill. When he turned back towards the window, the pavement outside the book shop was empty. There was no other word for Jeff's feelings at that moment than relief.

Outside, he crossed the road and took a look in the book shop window for himself. The shop was clearly going for a strong independent vibe, seeing its route to survival as providing an alternative, not direct competition, to the Waterstones on the town's main shopping square. An esoteric range of titles, almost entirely unfamiliar to Jeff, filled the window display. Curiosity piqued, he decided to investigate further. Jeff was one of those people who constantly promised himself that he would read more, and it suddenly occurred to him that this period of leave may be the perfect opportunity.

Inside, the wide variety of books continued. Fiction was on the first floor, so Jeff mounted the narrow, winding staircase and started to peruse the shelves. After a quick check of his favourite authors to see if any of them had put out anything new, he then started picking up books at random, scanning the backs to see what appealed.

The sound of footsteps made him look up. To his momentary horror, the pale young woman from outside appeared at the foot of a previously-unseen second set of stairs that led up to another floor that Jeff had not realised existed. He quickly diverted his gaze back to the cover of the book he was holding, hoping that his face wasn't reddening quite as much as it felt it was. He allowed himself another quick glance at the woman.

She stood just a few paces from him, also looking at the shelves in front of her. The crooked floorplan of the old building meant that the shelf she was looking at was at an odd angle to where Jeff stood, meaning the woman all but had her back to him. He shook his head to stop himself staring at her neck. There was something disconcerting about her, Jeff found, beyond his embarrassment at appearing to have followed her into the shop. He had no idea what it was, but now, this close to her, he felt distinctly uneasy. There was a familiarity, too, as if he had seen her before.

"This is not what you think it is."

Jeff started, nearly dropping the book he was holding. His head shot around, staring straight at the bookcase in front of him. She had caught him staring. Shit.

"I said, this is not what you think it is."

He didn't think it was anything, of course. Just two people in a bookshop. What did she think he thought it was?

He cleared his throat, anxiously. "No?"

There was no response. Turning around, he saw the woman was gone. The temptation to run down the stairs after her, to explain that he hadn't followed her into the shop, hadn't even realised she'd come in, was almost overwhelming. Fortunately, Jeff was too mortified to do so. He stood where he was for a few moments, then allowed himself to casually move over to the window to glance down at the street below. There was no sign of her outside. Downstairs, the bell over the door tinkled. Jeff stepped back from the window quickly, in case she appeared.

This is ridiculous, he thought. Yes, he'd noticed her from across the street. Yes, he'd experienced a momentary attraction to her. And yes, he'd contemplated following her into the book shop. But he'd also then decided firmly against it, hadn't realised she'd even entered the shop, and only come across out of an entirely innocent desire to buy a couple of books. He settled on his purchases and headed downstairs.

He refused to even let out a sigh of relief when the ground floor offered no sign of her.

Back at his flat, Jeff dropped the books he'd purchased on his kitchen worktop and made himself a cup of tea. The sense of achievement he'd felt that morning upon leaving the flat had vanished, quashed by the discomfort brought on by his non-encounter with the young woman.
He looked down at the two books he'd bought, a Dostoevsky and Stevenson's *Strange Case of Dr Jekyll and Mr Hyde*. He'd been standing by the Classics section when the woman had appeared and had clearly ended up buying the first two vaguely interesting titles that came to hand. He had actually been meaning to read *Jekyll and Hyde* for years, it had been one of his dad's favourites, but he was feeling too out of sorts to start something he assumed would be unsettling. He checked out the back of the Dostoevsky, but that, too, suddenly felt unnerving. He left the books where they were.

A few months prior, Jeff had bought himself a ticket to see a comedian at the Arts Centre in town. Now that the day had rolled around, the last thing he wanted to do was leave the flat. Unfortunately, he had told Anoush about the show during an argument they'd been having about how he never went out or did anything anymore, so Jeff knew for a fact that she would have made a note of it, with every intention of contacting him tomorrow to ask him how it was. He could lie, of course, but she'd know, of course. The last thing he needed was another row with his half-sister over her conviction that he was becoming a shut-in. Alas, the easiest thing to do would be to just go.
This was pretty much the only reason why, after a rather miserable heated-up ready meal, Jeff changed into a clean pullover and headed back outside. The Arts Centre

was only a short walk from his flat, which was something. Not only that, but it was a pleasant evening. It was dry, the sun was still out, and it was a reasonable temperature for a late summer evening. The Arts Centre had a small beer garden and was a popular hang-out for people even when not attending shows, so Jeff decided to set off early. There was always a chance that there would be someone there he knew. Hell, he might even text Anoush and see if she fancied meeting…

She must have sensed it for as he was thinking this, making his way from the bar outside to the garden, he felt the phone in his pocket buzzing. Pulling it out, he saw it was a text, from Anoush.

Hey babe, how r u? Up 2 much? Followed by the inevitable smiley face emoji.

Jeff cursed under his breath. She was as good as telling him that she remembered he was supposed to be going out, and that she also didn't expect him to be going. Sod you, he thought, sending her back a thumbs up emoji and then putting the phone back in his pocket. He took a swig of his drink and gave the beer garden a quick onceover. There was nobody around he recognised. Most of the people there were at least five or so years younger than him, he estimated. Ah well, it was a nice night. He took a seat at a table in a quiet corner of the garden and sat nursing his beer, watching the other patrons.

There was a group of four young people, in their early twenties, sitting at the next table over, and Jeff found himself watching them, marvelling at the oh-so-familiar dynamic being played out. Two girls, two boys. One of the girls more obviously attractive than the other, hoovering up most of the boys' attention. The other girl, skinny with black, lifeless hair in bunches was clearly, from what Jeff could hear, the smarter and funnier of the two young women. Yet she might as well have not been there so far as the boys were concerned. Jeff sighed.

Clearly, she would be much better company, and in a few years would have her choice of men as the vapid, short-lived appeal of her friend faded. He almost wanted to tell her that but was pretty sure she wouldn't want to hear it from some old random in a beer garden.

A bell sounded somewhere, the notification for ticketholders that the show was imminently about to start. Jeff, beer in hand, joined the exodus from the beer garden to take his place in the queue now forming at the auditorium doors. He filed in and, as the seating was unreserved, slipped into a seat on the end of a row at the back. Coming out to the show was one thing, but as soon as the (metaphorical, in this case) curtain came down, he wanted out of there. And besides, there was also no chance of being picked on this far back.

The group of four he'd been watching sat just a couple of rows in front of him. Unsurprisingly, the boys placed themselves either side of the attractive girl, the smarter one left on the outside like a spare appendage. Jeff shook his head as he took another sip of his beer. Kids. He leaned back into his chair and tried to make his legs disappear as someone squeezed past to get into the empty seat next to him, no doubt cursing him for not just getting up and moving along.

"I'm sorry?" Jeff had still been focused on the four youngsters, and so hadn't quite heard what the person next to him said.

"I said, this isn't what you think it is."

Jeff froze. He didn't turn to look at the person but kept his head facing firmly forward. Out of the corner of his eye, he could see a slim pair of legs in jeans, and an expensive looking pair of trainers.

"What did you say?" he whispered.

"This," said the voice. "Is not. What you think. It is."

Jeff felt his stomach churning, and the room started to swim. He caught a whiff of some unpleasant smell, acrid and oily, and put a hand out to steady himself on the back of the chair in front, causing the man sat there to turn round and glare at him. Jeff tried to apologise, even as he rose to his feet, but at that moment his knees buckled and his throat spasmed. He turned to the pale young woman in the seat next to him and was only just able to stop himself throwing up all over her. She was looking down at her phone, so Jeff was still unable to make out her face. He pushed back from his chair and into the aisle. Suddenly free of any support, he flailed around and immediately lost his balance.

"Oops, he's pissed!"

"Mate, get up!"

"Somebody ought to get him out of here!"

"Are you okay, mate?"

"Go on mate, off you trot!"

"Get him out of here!"

"Pisshead!"

"Get out!"

"Get out!"

"Get out!"

3

" **J**ezz! Come on! We've got to get out!"

Jeff shook his head, trying to clear the fog of pain away. His seat felt… wait, he wasn't in a seat, he was lying, reclining, on a floor. A metal floor? What the hell was going on?

"Jezz, man, we need to move!"

A bearded face was looking down at him, shouting in a Scandinavian accent over the chaotic sound of a straining engine, mixed with what sounded like gunfire. Jeff rolled onto his side and weakly spat a thick glob of phlegmy sputum onto the floor. He wiped a hand across his mouth, breaking the saliva string connecting his mouth to the floor.

"Teemu?" Jezz's brain struggled, reaching for a name for the beard that he knew he knew.

"Teemu, get him out, even if you have to drag him out! They're getting closer!"

"I know that, Price!" Teemu looked down at Jezz. "Come on, man, they'll be on top of us any minute."

Jezz looked around the tight confines of the tank. "Nora…?"

"She's outside, man, she's fine, she's spotting for us. Come on, buddy, we have to get out of here."

Jezz nodded, wincing as the pain in his arm flashed again. He was clutching it, he realised, blood running out over the hand that was holding the wound. "I'm okay, let's go."

Teemu's face broke out in relief, and he twisted and wormed his way through to the main chamber. Jezz, awkwardly, followed. There was an unfamiliar acrid, chemical smell in the tank that caught at the back of Jezz's throat, causing him to cough. Price patted him on the shoulder as he emerged into the command chamber and helped him up through the main hatch, following close behind. Teemu and Nora, out on the hull, pulled him out of the hatch. Nora gave him an anxious grin. "You had us worried there for a bit, soldier."

"What happened?"

"Phero-grenade. Lucky toss through the front hatch. The rest of us got our masks on in time, but you were too close to the discharge."

"How long was I out?"

"Just a few minutes," cut in Price, appearing from the hatch. "Which is about the amount of time we have now before we have bugs swarming all over us, so can we, pretty please, get the fuck out of here."

Nora and Teemu helped a still-shaky Jezz down off the hull. The tank was sitting in a plaza, smoke broiling from the rear. The buildings that surrounded them were scarred by heavy fighting, a couple of them partially collapsed. There was the chatter of gunfire close by to the west, probably only a few streets away. Two alien bodies lay nearby, the remains of the scout team that had disabled the tank. Jezz, still disorientated, stared at the bizarre, inhuman corpses. He shook his head to try and clear the fog as Teemu hoisted Jezz's good arm over his shoulder. Nora finished tying off the temporary dressing on his wound and the crew started off down the street they had rolled in from.

Nora led the way, her assault rifle at the ready, moving at a light jog. Teemu and Jezz followed, Jezz half stumbling, half pulled along by the bulky driver. The odour of the large man was almost choking Jezz at this proximity. It was bad enough sharing a tank with him. They'd have to say something when they got back, Jezz thought to himself as he stared down at his feet, trying to ensure he didn't trip and send them both flying. Price brought up the rear, his head constantly swinging round to check for signs of pursuit. They made their way like this for nearly half a mile along the deserted streets, with the ongoing sound of combat in their ears. Jezz's breathing grew ragged, and he was grateful when Teemu called for a break. Price, reluctantly, agreed and the crew took shelter in a burnt-out bakery. Price put Nora on the door, before swinging the pack off his shoulder and taking out the emergency radio.

"We're too far out and Jezz is too weak to go much further. I want a volunteer to stay here with him."

"Chief, you can't..."

"No arguments, Teemu. I'm signalling for an evac, but we've no idea whether there's any vehicle in the vicinity that can respond, or how long it might take. The four of us are sitting ducks here, and I'd much rather it was just two of us. Protocol is clear. In the event of our tank being disabled, our duty is to get back to base as soon as possible, as many of us as possible. I'd stay myself, you know that, but experienced tank commanders are thin on the ground and the orders on my returning as quickly as I'm able are unequivocal."

"Leave me with a gun and the pack," said Jezz. "One person can hide more effectively than two."

"Not happening. You took a phero-blast, you could fade out again any moment. That's if you don't just pass out. Then there's the arm wound."

Jezz grimaced. "The arm's fine. I caught it on something falling over in the tank. Not even anything, just a stupid accident."

"I'll stay." It was Nora who spoke. "Teemu's combat medicine skills aren't as up-to date as mine and, stupid accident or not, the arm's cut quite deeply. It needs to be kept an eye on. The two of you get back to base and we'll follow as soon as we're able. End of, Teemu."

The bearded driver looked uneasy, but he knew better than to argue with Nora. He eased Jezz to the floor. "Take it easy on him, Nora. You hang in there, buddy." He unslung his own weapon from his shoulder, checked it over once, then nodded at Price.

Price squatted down next to Jezz, his hand on the wounded man's shoulder. "Hang in there, Jezz. It's probably another mile back to base and if you're not picked up, then as soon as we're back, I'll get a vehicle and come back myself." He stared at him for a moment, willing Jezz to take in what he was saying. "And listen to Nora."

Jezz nodded. He watched as the two men made their way to the front of the building. Price briefly issued some last, whispered, orders to Nora. Jezz felt his eyelids getting heavy. By the time the door swung shut again behind Price and Teemu, he was out cold.

He was woken by Nora shaking him vigorously by the shoulder, one hand over his mouth. His eyes wide, he took a moment to remember where they were. Then he nodded at Nora. She slowly took her hand off his mouth. "You with me?" Her voice was low and carried an undertone of urgency.

Jezz nodded again. He was surprised to see how dark it was outside. He must have slept for a couple of hours, at least. He could hear still distant gunfire, but it was, if anything, further away than it had been.

"There's a patrol headed this way. I went out for a quick recce, nearly ran into them. They're not doing building-by-building, but we need to be ready."

"Okay." Jezz made to get up, Nora taking hold of his arm to help steady him. Together they made their way to the front of the store where Nora helped Jezz get comfortable behind the counter; far enough from the window to hopefully not be seen, but with a view out onto the street. Her black hair was roughly tied up and her face was streaked with camouflage face-paint. Handing Jezz a stick to apply his own, she took up a spot by the door. Jezz only had his revolver, which he checked over automatically. He then smeared some of the face-paint on. Shaking his head to try and clear the fog that was still clouding his thinking, he assumed an approximation of a state of readiness, vigilantly watching the street.

There was torchlight. Nora signalled at him, but Jezz had seen it too. He took up a firing position, focusing his attention on the beams of light that were sweeping the street outside, one eye on Nora for the Go Hot signal.

The patrol was in sight now. Between their searchlights and the diffused light from other sources, Jeff could make out the unsettling, alien outlines of their enemy as they made their way along the street in the direction of the bakery. He was anxious to know if Nora thought this was a routine patrol or if they were looking for them, but he knew that any noise now could get them killed. Nora wouldn't be looking for a firefight. Things would go much better for them if the patrol went past and never saw them. Luckily, so far, it didn't look like they were entering any of the buildings, merely sweeping their searchlights over windows and doorways. Jezz leaned back further into the shadows, trying hard to keep his breathing under control.

Shit. The patrol stopped, seemingly to discuss their next course of action, just a few yards from the bakery door. The hideous, alien buzzing of their chatter set Jezz's teeth on edge, and the way their mandibles clattered made the bile rise up his throat. The tension was unbearable. Then the chatter stopped; the inside of the bakery was suddenly lit up by searchlights. The flash of light was momentary, passing before Jezz could even think to hold his breath. Neither Nora or Jezz was picked out. The alien patrol moved on.

It was around midnight when Nora helped Jezz down from the armoured half-track that had picked them up. Despite the late hour, and the fact that the snow had started again, the temporary camp set up in parkland in Shapingba district was abuzz with activity. Soldiers running back and forth delivering orders, mechanics working on vehicles under floodlights, a constant hum of engine noise. Shouting could be heard from all over; orders, complaints, insults both good-natured and less so. Jezz paid all of it no mind as Nora supported him and they started to walk. Thank God she smelled better than Teemu, Jezz thought, though, as he was forced to admit to himself, the difference was not as much as he expected.

They had seen no further signs of enemy troops, other than the constant background chatter of gunfire across the city, and Jezz had even managed to get some more sleep on the drive back. He was ashen, though, as Nora helped him into the med-centre. After a quick physical exam, where they redressed his wound and gave him as clean a bill of health as they could, he was passed on to the psych team.

"So you took the full blast of a phero-grenade?" The doctor was a thin, tired looking man in his late-fifties perched on a stool, currently staring down at a clipboard as he sipped a mug of hot coffee. Jezz hadn't seen him around the base before, but that was no surprise. All the med teams were pretty much constantly busy, and this was Jezz's first exposure to the aliens' chemical warfare technology.

From where Jezz was sat on a gurney, he had the height advantage, and he stared down at the doctor's scalp through his thinning hair. He grunted his assent. The doctor took another sip of coffee.

"What did you experience?"

Jeff didn't answer immediately, wary of being marked unfit for combat. He realised, though, that the doctor wasn't going to be dissuaded from his enquiries so easily. "Old times, civilian stuff, before the war. I don't know, I guess, thirty, forty years ago? I don't know where I was, but it was warm, and I was just... I don't know, relaxing, walking around a city? It wasn't me, though. I didn't feel like... me."

"How long?"

"My crew said I was out for a few minutes..."

"And how long did it seem to you, in the hallucination?"

"Oh, I don't know. A day, I guess? It was certainly a number of hours."

The doctor scribbled down a few notes. "And since you've come back, any recurrence?"

"No."

"Visual anomalies of any sort? Things in this world that looked like they might be manifestations from the hallucination?"

Jezz remembered the civilian he thought he'd seen behind the alien scout that had... but no, that was before the phero-grenade, so that can't have been...

"Nope. Nothing."

"And have you slept?"

"A couple of times, not for long. While we were waiting to get picked up."

"Dreams?"

"Not that I can remember."

The doctor paused. For the first time, he looked up at Jezz, a thoughtful expression on his face. After a few seconds he asked, "You feel alright, soldier?"

"I'm exhausted. But yeah, I guess, I don't feel... weird or anything. Yeah."

The doctor stood up and put the clipboard down on his desk. "Sounds like you were lucky. If there's any recurrence, any at all; if you see things, hear things, anything, report it. Other than that, I'd say you need a decent night's sleep and then you'll be back out there. How's the arm?"

"Flesh wound. Got to keep it dressed but it won't keep me out of combat."

"Good." The doctor nodded. "Get out of my office then." He gave Jezz a pat on the shoulder as the tankman eased himself off the bed and gently yet firmly pushed him out through the door, shutting it behind him.

The decent night's sleep the doctor prescribed was not forthcoming. Not that Jezz had expected it to be. Their battalion had been immersed in heavy combat since they arrived in Chongqing and it was around six in the morning when Jezz was roused from his bed by Teemu, bearing coffee. The bearded driver helped Jezz to his feet and the two of them stepped outside their tent. Jezz, like the rest of his company, had slept in his clothes for weeks. For all his bitching about Teemu's rank body odour, he realised this morning that his was no better. Teemu lit two cigarettes and passed one to Jezz.

"Briefing in thirty fuck minutes. Never let us fuck rest for a minute."

Jezz nodded in reply. "They get our ride back?"

"Recovery team wheeled it in at about four. Price is over there now, giving mechanics hell no doubt." Teemu let out a single bark of laughter, pleased for once that it was someone else getting shit from Price.

"So, we heading back out there?"

"Fuck do I know?" Teemu threw the rest of his coffee into the mud before tossing the mug back through the tent's doorway onto his bed. "Come on, I need piss."

Jezz trotted behind the big man, flexing his arm and trying to get some life back into his shoulder as they stamped over to the latrine. "Get me some breakfast," grunted the driver. "I'm heading to the whizz palace."

Teemu peeled off, leaving Jezz on his own to forage something to eat from what passed for a mess.

"Hey buddy," said Nora, slapping him on his bad arm, making him wince, as she came up behind him. "Where you headed?"

"Get Teemu some breakfast, then the briefing I guess."

Nora looked at her watch. "No breakfast for you, my man, briefing starts in three."

"Shit," Jezz rolled his eyes. "Teemu said we had half an hour."

"Teemu has no concept of time, you know that. Come on."

They were amongst the last to arrive, taking up seats at the back. Price slipped into the seat next to them just as Colonel Holt marched into the briefing room. "Where the hell is Teemu?" he whispered, his usual angry undertone barely under control.

"I was making a piss," whispered Teemu as he sat down. He leaned past Price and addressed Jezz. "Where's my breakfast?"

"I didn't have time to get breakfast, you idiot…"

They were cut off by the Colonel banging his baton on the table in front of the rows of seats, bringing the assembled vehicle crews to order.

"Listen up. We're heading back out there today, and I want everything you've got. The remnants of the 86th are pinned down in Dashiba District to the North, crying out to be relieved, so we need to break though the Eltiy'ch line and get to them before they're crushed." He moved around the table to position himself beside the map posted on the display board behind. "The weakest areas, so far as we can tell are here, here and here." Each 'here' was punctuated by his baton smacking the map, like an army colonel from a movie. "We'll break the company into three prongs, and attack simultaneously, with a fourth detachment of light Humvees held in reserve to support as necessary. Now, before…"

Before he could even get to the end of that sentence, it transpired. Major Blunt suddenly appeared at the door and hurried over to the Colonel, whispering urgently under his breath. He didn't stop for some time, only pausing while Holt fired back his own muffled questions. The men at the front strained to hear, the ones at the back started to mutter amongst themselves. Something was up.

"Well shit," Holt said finally, this time loud enough to be heard by the men. Something in his frame seemed to slump as he placed his baton down on the table. He stood there for a moment, his face grey. He looked as if he had aged ten years in the few minutes since Blunt appeared. "Belie those orders, men. You're to return to your quarters now and get ready to mobilise. We're withdrawing. The whole division."

A wave of unease rolled out over the room, the crews staring at each other in confusion.

"I want the entire camp packed up and ready to move out in three hours. No excuses. What we can't take, we leave. Tank crews, stay here for further orders. The rest of you, dismissed."

There was a low chorus of urgent chatter as the main bulk of the attending personnel filed out. After they'd gone, the tank crews moved forward. Holt perched on the side of the table, waiting until the last departing soldier had left before saying anything.

"It's a shitshow, men. In the early hours of this morning, the Eltiy'ch launched a coordinated surprise attack on five of our air bases. It was a total wipeout. As of 0400 hours this morning, we have no air support available for three hundred miles. I don't need to tell you that without air support, our ground operations are fucked. We're pulling out of the entire Chongqing area, and back into Sichuan Province. With air support gone, the Eltiy'ch's control of the skies will give them further control over the weather. Temperatures are already dropping. The clock is ticking, we're in a race to get out before our vehicles become inoperable."

Jezz, Teemu and Nora shared an uneasy glance.

"Is three hours realistic for a safe evac?" Price, ever the realist.

Holt sighed wearily. "I don't know. Probably not. Which is why I've kept you back. We've just sixteen tanks left operational…"

"Seventeen, sir. Captain Price's was recovered last night and should be running again in the next forty minutes." This was Travers, the lead tank engineer.

Holt nodded. "Good. Seventeen tanks then. These machines are vital, they're proving to be the most efficient of our armoured firepower in the low temperatures, hence why the bugs are so keen on targeting them." He glanced around at the officers in front of him, swiftly making eye contact with each of them. When he spoke again, his voice brooked no argument. "We cannot afford to lose these vehicles. I want you on the Ziyang road within the hour."

"But sir, that'll leave the rest of the battalion critically exposed…" Captain Huang, one of the other tank commanders.

Holt, a haunted look in his eyes, stood up, pulling at his tunic as he did so. "We cannot afford to lose the tanks," he repeated. "Within the hour, men."

He left the room. Nobody mentioned the 86th, now left to try and break out on their own.

*   *   *

Jezz would never forget the looks on the faces of the soldiers in camp as they paused in their preparations to watch the column of tanks roll out. He was stood in the front hatch, making the most of the fresh air, and had his goggles on, mainly to avoid making inadvertent eye contact with anyone. Soldiers, mechanics and other personnel stood to watch them roll by. Some offered salutes, a few offered middle fingers, and/or barbed jibes. Most just stared. Exhausted looking men and women in filthy fatigues; pale, thin walking corpses, most of them. The strategic necessity of preserving their tank capability wasn't lost on any of the troops watching them leave, but they also knew that the fact they were being left to make their own way with Half-tracks and Humvees, without air support, was little short of a death sentence. The mood was grim.

It was snowing lightly but Holt was right, temperatures were already dropping. Jezz hoped the three hours the rest of the company had been given could be brought down to two. He offered a forlorn wave to the doctor who'd carried out his psych exam, as the man paused from loading medical supplies onto a truck to watch the column pass. The doctor nodded, his arms weighed down with kit. As Jezz started to bring his arm down he froze. Behind the doctor, between a pair of tents, he caught a glimpse of a pale young woman watching them from behind a tent, her short, cropped hair a vivid white. The doctor frowned at Jezz's reaction, but the column rolled on and Jezz quickly lost sight of the pair.

"You okay, Jezz?" Nora was stood in the main hatch, where Price would usually be, except the captain was down in the chamber, going over maps.

Jezz didn't respond for a moment, his arm still halfway down from saluting the doctor. Then he shook his head, rubbing his face vigorously to try to bring himself back to the present. "Yeah, I'm... Yeah. Fine." He faced front again and took out a pack of cigarettes to distract himself. Lighting one, exhaling a cloud of smoke almost indistinguishable from the exhalation of breath in the cold temperatures, he shook his head again. Forget it, he thought. Aftershock from the phero-grenade. You're tired, but the doc said you were okay. You slept normally, it's no big thing.

The morning was quiet, no sign of any Eltiy'ch forces. Despite the light snow it was a sunny day, and for the rest of the morning they made good time. Roads were clear and the odd obstacle they came across, debris, fallen trees, abandoned vehicles, were soon removed. Officially, there were no civilians left in the combat zone, or indeed in Chongqing in general. Waves of refugees had flooded into neighbouring provinces as soon as the Eltiy'ch had first landed, and from there south into Myanmar and Bangladesh. But everyone knew, of course, that you could never totally evacuate an entire population. Sure enough, every now and then on the road north, Jezz would catch sight of a local, or a small group of them, peeking out from one of the more intact buildings, or maybe foraging in abandoned supermarkets. Sometimes they would even catch sight of children, playing the in rubble. Whereas the adults usually looked away, or watched with a surly detachment, the children often stopped what they were doing and waved at the tanks, some even running up to the side of the road. Price reminded them grimly not to encourage this, not even to return their waves. This was standard protocol. Nobody wanted to be the reason a child was shot by some Eltiy'ch marksman hiding in a nearby building. But it saddened Jezz that he couldn't offer these kids some gesture of kindness, even just a nod or a salute.

At midday, Nora hopped down onto the hull of the tank with two bowls of steaming noodles. She perched next to where Jezz stood in the hatch and passed him one of the bowls. "You doing okay there?"

Jezz nodded, flicking the tail end of the cigarette he'd been smoking away. He took the bowl. "Cheers. What is it?"

"Chicken." Nora poked at her bowl with her fork. "At least, Price says it's chicken. Who the fuck knows what he's basing that on."

Jezz forked a helping of noodles into his mouth, grimacing slightly. They were passing through a more open area of wasteland now; deserted factories stood rotting amongst wide open tarmacked areas that had presumably at one time been loading areas and lorry parks. Grass was breaking through the concrete, covered as it was by a light smattering of snow turning to slush in the sun. Clearly this area had already been on its arse long before the Eltiy'ch had showed up. They were more exposed here, but with the buildings being further away, they were also less susceptible to snipers. In any event, they were heading further from the front line. At least so far as you could define a line in the protracted street-to-street battle of Chongqing. But the column was relaxed, and most tanks had one or two crew out on the hull, making the most of the sun, despite still being bundled up against the artificial cold brought on by the Eltiy'ch atmosphere manipulators.

Nora indicated a group of around a couple of dozen civilians tramping down a sideroad towards the highway. "Looks like this lot are giving up the ghost and finally getting out of here."

"I shouldn't imagine we're the only company who's on the move. They must realise Chongqing's lost and it's time to get out."

"The time to get out was three months ago, the fucking idiots." Nora was Chinese-American, and as such seemed to feel she had more right to be scathing about the local

Chinese than any of her comrades did. Jezz wasn't sure it worked like that, but the crew had learned to let it pass.

As the column grew closer, the group became more distinct. "I count twenty, no, twenty-one," said Nora, before slurping at another mouthful of her noodles.

"Yep, I... no, twenty-two..." Jezz nearly dropped his fork, as in the middle of the crowd he suddenly saw a flash of white amongst the dingy clothing of the refugees. He dropped his bowl through the hatch and reached down for his rifle.

"What the hell, Jezz?"

"Take cover!" he yelled, flicking the safety off on his rifle and bringing it round to bear on the group.

"What's going on? Jezz?" Price popped his head up from the main hatch.

Jezz didn't answer as his rifle swung back and forth, trying to locate the pale young woman in the midst of the group. The tank in front of them, hearing the shouting, slowly brought its turret around to face the group, followed in turn by the tank in front of it. Nora could hear the tanks behind them following suit.

"Jezz! What's going on!" Price's voice was insistent, his moustache quivering. The last thing they needed was a group of civilians mowed down because of a jittery tank crew. He had a radio handset in his hand. "Hold fire! Hold fire!" he barked into it.

Jezz was out of his hatch now, stood perched on the hull, Nora crouched at his feet with her rifle also covering the group. "Talk to me Jezz," she shouted. "Talk to me."

As the column rolled on down the highway, Jezz's tank drew level with the junction with the sideroad that the civilians were tramping down. The civilians had stopped now, about a couple of hundred feet from the junction. They were visibly terrified, and a couple looked like they were about to run for it. Others in the group grabbed at them, aware that any sudden movement now would trigger a shower of bullets and shells to rain down on them.

"I can't see her! I can't see her!" Jezz was almost screaming.

Price, finally figuring out what was happening, shouted down to Nora. "For fuck's sake get him down and get that rifle off him." He barked into the radio again. "Hold fire, hold fire. I repeat, do not engage."

Nora shouldered her weapon and stood up, slowly but firmly pushing the barrel of Jezz's rifle down towards the ground. Then, taking his face in both hands, she turned his head round so he was looking at her. "Jezz. It's okay. It's Nora. You're okay. They're human. Just civilians." Eyes wide open, he didn't seem to recognise her. "They're just civilians, Jezz. You're okay."

The refugees watched in confusion and fear as the last of the tanks rolled past. They didn't start to move again until the column was some way down the highway. Jezz was now sat on the hull, with Nora squatting down next to him, checking him over, a concerned expression on her face. He looked stunned but was starting to come round.

"What happened, Jezz?"

"I thought... I thought I saw her."

"Who did you see, Jezz?"

"The woman..." He looked up at Nora, blinking wildly as his brain caught up with reality. "The woman I saw in my vision, the phero-grenade. There was a young woman, really pale, hair almost white, in the other place. I thought I saw her in that group of... Shit, what did I do, Nora?" A wave of nausea crashed over Jezz as he pictured the civilians scattered, as corpses, across the road. He half-gagged, half-coughed, and spat out a mouthful of thick saliva onto the tarmac.

"It's fine, nothing happened. They're okay. A few of them probably pissed themselves, but nothing happened, it's okay."

"How are we doing down there?" Price, from the main hatch.

"We're good, captain. We're calm, it's okay."

"Get him down in the hold, give him something to help him sleep. I think we can manage for a few hours from here without him." Price was speaking from between gritted teeth, clearly fighting back the urge to tear into Jezz.

Nora nodded as she helped Jezz to his feet. They mounted the turret and she helped him down the hatch, following him down and tucking him up in a corner. Breaking out a med-pack, she handed him a couple of pills and a bottle of water. "Take these, buddy. There you go."

Jezz took the pills and shut his eyes…

4

"Mmmhmm, hmm…wha…?"

He struggled for breath, a great weight on his chest.

"Jeff, wake up! Wake up!"

A burst of chatter in his ears, then the sound of people straining, at the same time as the sensation of being lifted. Jezz didn't open his eyes, but he could tell there was a strong light very close. This was wrong, there's minimal lighting in the tank… What's going on?

"Jeff? Jeff? Can you hear me, love? It's Anoush…"

"Jeffrey, it's Doctor Singh, can you hear me? You're okay, Jeffrey. Everything's okay. Can you hear me?"

Whoever was lifting him set him down on a soft surface, a bed? He hadn't been in a proper bed for weeks. 'Doctor Singh'. Was he in a hospital? Were they in Ziyang already? Jezz opened one eye, slowly, just enough to get a sense of the room. A familiar looking woman was leaning over him, her face full of concern.

"Nora?"

"Jeff? I don't know who that is. It's me, Jeff, it's Anoush. It's your sister."

"Anoush?" Jeff opened his other eye, staring up at the pinched, tired face of his half-sister. "Anoush, where am I?"

"It's okay, Jeff. You're in Gilder Ward. You had a blackout."

"What, where… I was at the theatre…"

"Yes, Jeffrey, that's right. You were at the theatre, when you started shouting out some very strange things and seemed to be out of step with reality. Were you hallucinating?"

Jeff rolled his head over to look at the doctor on the other side of the bed. "Doctor Singh! Yes, I… yes, I was… somewhere else. What's happened?"

"It's alright, Jeffrey, we just had to help you back into bed. You were thrashing around in a confused state when you woke up and fell out of bed, but I don't think you've hurt yourself."

"How long have I been here?"

"It's been a couple of days, Jeff," answered Anoush. "You haven't been yourself since you arrived. It's good to see you recognise us again."

"What's going on…?"

"Jeffrey, I advise you try and go back to sleep for now. We'll have a talk about this later, when you've recovered a bit, but for now I need to speak to your sister."

Jeff laid his head back on the pillow and closed his eyes.

Jeff stayed in hospital for the next two days, slowly coming back round to some level of normality. Anoush visited him each afternoon, bringing messages of support from his stepmother. Their father had died several years previously, and Anoush had worked hard at keeping the familial relationship intact. Jeff's relationship with his stepmother, Anya, had never been particularly close, and when Jack died, Jeff hadn't seen Anya for three years. It had been Anoush who had reached out to her brother, slowly bringing him back into the fold. Anya's willingness to have him back in her life had shamed Jeff at first, conscious as he was of the brattish way he'd reacted to his widowed father's new wife. She was, he had learned the hard way, a good woman and one who believed in family. Even when some might feel they had no connection left, she looked out for him as if he were her own, as did Anoush. Though Anoush's concern could sometimes manifest itself with a certain waspishness.

She was certainly a touch frosty in the car driving him back to his flat. "When did you stop taking your medication then?"

"I don't remember, I don't think I did."

"Doctor Singh doesn't seem to think there's any other reason for the relapse."

"I'm not sure it was a relapse. It felt... different. Felt very real."

Jeff looked out of the window and for a moment, he experienced the involuntary visualisation of a young Chinese woman's face. Inexplicably, he put the name Nora to the face.

"Jeff, we're worried about you. You have to promise me to start taking your meds again."

"Anoush, I will. I am. Can we stop here?"

"What? What for?"

"I just want to get cigarettes."

"You're smoking again?"

Was he? Jeff felt a moment of confusion. "I... no, it's okay. No, of course."

Anoush took her eye off the road for a moment to look at him. "Jeff, I honestly don't think you ought to be at the flat on your own at the moment," she said, returning her concentration to the traffic.

"Anoush, I can't go back to Anya's. Your mother's very kind..."

"She's your mother too."

"Sorry, yes, I know, all right. Anya's lovely, but she'll smother me, and I need to try and clear my head."

"Then don't go to hers, come and stay with me."

"Stay with you?"

"Why not? Phil's moved out…"

"Phil's moved out?"

"Is there an echo in here?"

"An echo?"

For the first time on the drive, Anoush almost smiled as she took a hand momentarily off the wheel to smack him in the chest. "It's nothing, a tantrum. Or maybe not. I don't know. Or care, frankly. The point is, he's not there. I'm working from home a lot, but I'd be in the study. You'd have to sleep on the couch, but you'd have the living room to yourself during the day. I can cook for you. It's been so long since I've seen you, it'd be good for us to spend some time together. Besides, with Phil gone, I could use the company."

They pulled up outside Jeff's flat and Anoush turned the engine off, twisting in her seat to look at Jeff straight on. He was reminded, as he always was when he looked at her, of their father, their one genetic link. Anoush was, largely, her mother's daughter. Same dirty blonde hair, same pinched, thin features. But her eyes were Jack's. Jeff scratched his ear to distract himself. "Okay. Just let me go in and get a few things."

"You want a hand?"

"No, I'm good, won't take long."

"Okay."

Anoush watched Jeff get out and go up to his building. He gave her a half-hearted wave as he pulled the door closed behind him.

Jeff climbed the stairs to the first floor and unlocked the door to his flat. The noise alerted Chris, his neighbour, and the door to the next flat opened. Chris, overweight, curly haired and, good grief, in a vest, shorts and robe even though it was, Jeff checked, two in the afternoon, appeared, holding a pot of instant noodles.

"Jeff."

"Hey Chris. Not at work?"

"No, you?"

"No, I've been… few days off."

"Me too. Wanna come over later? I've had a couple of new Korean horror films arrive, we could make a night…"

"No, Chris." Jeff was in no mood to play along with Chris' mates-y chuntering. "Look, I'm staying with my sister for a bit. Her husband's left her again. I'm just collecting a few things."

"Anoush is here?" Chris peered over the landing.

"Outside in the car. Chris, I've got to get on." Jeff was exhausted and talking to Chris never made him feel any better at the best of times.

"Okay, Jeff. I'll catch you later." Another peek over the landing, and Chris retreated into his flat. Jeff sighed with relief.

He went inside his own flat and shut the door, leaning back on it for a moment while he yawned and wondered what the heck he was doing. Moving in with Anoush was crazy, and he should know, he thought whimsically. She'd be all over him, nagging him out of sisterly love, driving him up the wall within a week, no doubt. He pushed himself off the door and opened a drawer in his kitchenette, retrieving a pack of emergency cigarettes he kept hidden there. Lighting one, he went over to the living area and dropped down onto the couch. Anoush could wait ten minutes, he was sure.

He nearly flipped on the tv, but realised if he got sucked into anything, Anoush would soon be banging on his door, and she would not appreciate the necessity of coming up to drag him out. Scowling at the taste and remembering why he quit, he took a last drag on the cigarette before dropping it, half-smoked, into an abandoned cup of tea, and pushed himself up off the sofa. Grabbing a rucksack out of the cupboard in his bedroom, he threw a few clothes in it, collected a handful of books and his iPad, then stood in the middle of the living area again, looking around at the unremarkable collection of objects that made up his life. Five minutes throwing a few bits and pieces in a bag and he could now quite happily not come back for anything for a few months. Was he losing it, or is this just what happens when you reach a point where there's no 'it' to lose? He checked all the windows, turned the thermostat down on his heating, grabbed a couple of bits from the fridge that wouldn't last and headed out. Locked the door, checked it, and shuffled down the stairs.

Anoush looked around at him as he threw his rucksack on the back seat.

"All set?"

Jeff clambered into the passenger seat and shut the door. "Yup."

He put the pint of milk he was donating along with some cheese in the fridge, took the books out of his rucksack and placed them on the coffee table, then stowed the rucksack down beside Anoush's sofa.

"Make yourself at home, Jeff. You want a cup of tea?"

"Sure, yeah. Okay." Jeff sat down on the sofa and flicked on the tv. Late afternoon, so quiz shows. That was okay, he could handle that. His attention wandered from the show almost as soon as he put it on. He cast an eye round the living room, taking in the bookshelf with the huge array of crime and sci-fi novels on it. "Phil didn't take his books then?"

Anoush came into the room, set two mugs of tea down and then wandered through into the bedroom. "No," she called out behind her. "As usual I'm just left here looking at his shit while he cries into his beer at one of his idiot friends' houses, no doubt telling them all what a bitch I am."

Jeff, who naturally loved his half-sister, wondered again at the tragic twist of fate that had thrown her together with Phil, one of the weakest individuals Jeff had ever met. Her natural instinct was to bully. Out of love, granted, but bully nevertheless. Life was a constant stream of black/white, yes/no decisions to Anoush and she didn't hesitate to tell the men in her life, Jeff, Phil, her business partner Ranjit, what those decisions should be. Phil had just enough backbone that every now and then he fled, usually in tears, from the despotic rule of his well-intentioned wife.

Anoush came back into the room, having changed into an absurdly uncharacteristic onesie, decorated in the white and black patches of a Friesian cow. She reached behind her, tying her blonde hair up as she plumped down on the couch next to her brother. She raised her feet up onto the sofa, looked at Jeff and then leant over and rested her head on his shoulder.

"I was so worried about you, honey. We both were." 'Both' meaning her and Anya, Jeff realised, not her and Phil. Jeff had only met Phil a handful of times. They had not bonded. The one thing Jeff really didn't get about him was how Phil couldn't understand that Anoush was driven purely by a desire for the people around her to be better, for their own sakes. Her methods were at times abrasive, but Phil really couldn't have a more loving or supportive wife. He was just too fragile to be loved like that.

"I know," he replied. Anoush sat up straight again, allowing Jeff to lean forward and take something out of his satchel that Anoush had brought from the hospital. He put his medication on the table. "Look, I haven't just abandoned my meds. I'm pretty sure I didn't stop taking them. I may have missed the odd day here and there, but I'm not derailing." He sat back. "Not like that, at least."

Anoush picked up the packet. "Of course, I don't know when you started this pack. So…"

"Yeah, yeah. But I had it on me, is the point. That was in my satchel, I didn't pick it up at home. So I'm keeping it on me. If it makes you feel better, take it. Administer it, while I'm here.

Anoush looked at him, lips pursed, then handed the medication back to him. "No, it's okay. I need to trust you."

"Yeah, you bloody do," Jeff smiled at her, receiving a playful punch in return. "Now, you still using Phil's Netflix login? I feel like ruining his algorithms."

Anoush laughed, and Jeff grinned as he felt a slight stab of pain in his heart.

It was his father's laugh.

It transpired that Anoush had already rung Graham, Jeff's boss, and made arrangements for his absence. Some men might be annoyed at the interference, but Jeff had learned long ago to live with it and, frankly, at the moment he'd take any excuse to not do anything. Graham knew Anoush, of course. You couldn't know Jeff without knowing Anoush, so there was no argument from that end. Graham texted Jeff, just to see how he was, to reassure him that work had him covered for the time Doctor Singh had signed him off, and that they'd talk in a couple of weeks.

Anoush kept her promise and, though working from home, left Jeff alone during the day. He didn't venture far from the flat, other than picking up groceries for them, which also allowed him to sneak the odd cigarette. The rest of the time he spent either reading or watching tv with the sound down low. The next few days passed in a haze of inactivity. He grew addicted to antique shows, braving Anoush's scorn by making her watch them as they ate the lunches he made, and made some serious advances through Mervyn Peake's *Gormenghast*, which he'd been meaning to read for years and never gotten around to. In the evenings, he and Anoush watched movies and played boardgames, reliving to a certain degree Anoush's later teens, when he'd still been at home, finishing his degree at the local university. Jeff felt vaguely guilty that he might be keeping Anoush from her social life, but on the third night, after a bottle and a half of wine, she'd broken down and admitted that there really wasn't much of one these days. Her friends had drifted away when she'd married Phil and most of their circle was now made up of his friends. Friends that, whenever Phil had one of his episodes and walked out, tended to close ranks and side with him. Carole, her closest friend, was in South America at the moment and so Anoush confessed that she really had invited Jeff as much for her own sake as for his. Jeff, for his part, was glad he'd agreed to stay, and decided there and then that he wouldn't return home at the first opportunity. Maybe it would be good for him and Anoush to get closer again. After all, as refreshing as it had been (before it all turned psychotic), if the day of his attack had shown him anything, it was that his own social life was hardly in great shape. And living here for a bit would keep him away from Chris for a while. A win all round, frankly.

They two of them sat on the couch, Anoush in her onesie and Jeff in jeans and a clean t-shirt, watching a Mark Duplass movie. Jeff had his arm around his sister, slightly against his will, but for all her spiky personality, Anoush was big on physical expression of familial love. He felt for the first time in a long while relaxed, truly relaxed. It would take a lot, he thought, to unsettle him tonight. Something like a familiar, pale woman appearing in the background of the movie they were watching. He tried not to react, but Anoush clearly felt him tense up.

"Jeff, what's wrong?"

"No… nothing. No, I'm fine. I…"

She sat up and looked at him, reaching for the controls and pausing the film. "Jeff, what is it?"

Jeff rubbed his eyes, screwed them up in an almost cartoon-ish show of disbelief at what he'd seen, and looked back at the tv. There was no sign of the woman. He leaned forward and put his glass on the table.

"It's nothing. Cramp."

Anoush continued to stare at him for a moment, before sitting back and putting Jeff's arm around her shoulder again. Jeff said nothing, just restarted the movie.

The sound of a clarinet playing could be heard coming from an open window at the front of the house as Anoush and Jeff started up the driveway. Jeff assumed it was Anya playing, until the piece suddenly went awry with a succession of bum notes before grinding to a halt. Anoush winced. "Mum's still giving lessons on Wednesdays and Thursdays." She glanced at her watch, "She should be finishing up soon."

Anoush had her own keys, so they let themselves in and slipped into the kitchen. Their arrival was noted, if not reacted to, by a ball of orange fluff reclining sedately on the kitchen worktop. "Hey, Giora." Jeff leant up against the work surface and started to stroke the cat. Anoush bared her teeth at Giora as she reached for the kettle. Anoush was not a cat person. Giora, as always, ignored both of them equally.

"Tea?"

Jeff nodded, his attention entirely on the soft ginger fur he was sinking his hand into.

The clarinet playing, which had resumed, stumbled to a conclusion. Anya's voice, though indistinct, could be heard coming from the front room. Presumably giving a last few notes to her student before dismissing them. A few moments later, Jeff and Anoush looked up as Anya entered the kitchen.

"Jeffrey! My darling!" Anya, thin as a rake with a huge mass of thick, curly hair, reached out for her stepson and drew him into a tight hug. Other than Doctor Singh, Anya was the only person who still called him Jeffrey. "I was so worried when Anoush told me what had happened. My God, what on earth is going on with you?"

"Hey, Anya." Jeff returned the hug gently, afraid as always that any tighter and he might break the stick-like figure in his arms. As fragile as she seemed physically, however, he was, as always, struck by the palpable air of *life* that his stepmother exuded.

He found himself looking over Anya's shoulder at a teenage girl, dressed in jeans and a hoodie and holding a clarinet case, head bowed, her straggly red hair hanging over her heavy-lidded eyes. The girl's face was a mass of freckles. Jeff coughed.

"Oh shit, where are my manners?" Anya released Jeff and turned around, gesturing at the girl. "Jeffrey, Anoush, this is Sophie. Sophie, these are my children Anoushka and Jeffrey. Come to visit their dear mother, *finally*."

"Hello Sophie," Anoush peered disinterestedly over the rim of her mug.

The girl raised a hand, "Hey."

"Darlings, I was just going to run Sophie home…"

"It's okay, Mrs Ginetti, I can get a bus, the 86 stops at the end of the road in ten minutes."

"Well, if you're sure, darling, but I'm going to text your mother to make sure she's okay with that." Anya's phone was already out, looking down as she typed with both thumbs. Clearly she didn't need to be talked into letting the girl make her own way.

"Okay, so I'm gonna go…"

"Good, good… Oh, Sophie," Anya looked up and the girl turned back to look over her shoulder, "Don't forget,

I want you to practice the Mozart concerto, the second movement."

"Yes, Mrs Ginetti." Sophie was out in the hallway by this point and her final farewell was delivered just as she opened the door. It slammed behind her.

"Lovely girl, lousy clarinettist." Anya put her phone in her back pocket and turned back to Jeffrey. "Really, darling, what's going on, are you off your meds again?"

Jeff gave Giora a final scratch behind the ears then picked up his tea. "I don't know, Anya. I'm sure I've been taking them, but it's been a bit of a blur. I don't know if I've been working too hard. Graham had to make me take some time off recently, so maybe he could see I wasn't doing so great. I don't know."

Anya looked at him for a moment, a sad bemused look in her eye, then she reached out and hugged him again. "You're staying for dinner, my darlings, yes?"

Anoush rolled her eyes and Jeff grinned. "Where are ordering from tonight, mother?"

Anya stepped back and pinched Jeff's cheek. "I always know I'm being sassed when you call me 'mother'. Pizza's on you, you little putz."

Jeff still couldn't reconcile how comfortable being around these two women made him feel these days, given how long it had taken him to get over what he had seen as Jack's betrayal in wanting another family. But evenings spent in the company of the effusive, wild-haired and slightly eccentric klezmer musician and her sardonic, brittle yet loving daughter never failed to make him feel like he was home. Anya liked an open fire, always starting them far earlier in the year than was necessary, so the three of them sat around a Scrabble board with a bottle of wine and the crackling of the fire for company. A Giora Fiedman record on the stereo completed the mood, the master clarinettist's namesake curled up on Jeff's lap, ignoring the occasional glare thrown his way by Anoush.

The younger woman was narrowly beating her mother, with Jeff merely making up the numbers. Often the two women would gang up on him if made a particularly poor play, berating and mocking him in equal measure. "You don't try, darling, that's the problem. You could be so much better at this if you just tried." Jeff shrugged. Winning never seemed that important to him, he just liked their company.

They shared the usual jokes, the usual memories of Jack, and for a couple of hours Jeff managed to forget the pale young woman and the chaotic episodes of the past few days. He drank sparingly and when, as Anoush declared victory, there was talk of another bottle of wine being opened, he declined. Instead, he got up to help himself to a non-alcoholic beer that he knew he'd find in the fridge.

Anya followed him out into the kitchen, brandishing a packet of cigarettes. "I know what you're doing!" called Anoush from the front room.

"For God's sake, I'm nearly sixty, darling, I'll smoke a cigarette if I want one!" Anya raised her eyebrows at Jeff, shaking the packet at him. He nodded, opening his beer and following his stepmother out onto the patio.

It was fully nighttime now, and there was little light other than the moon. Anya's musical career had been sporadically lucrative, and she and Jack had managed to purchase a house in a very nice part of town; large garden, little in the way of night-time noise or activity. Hedgehogs often visited the garden, and it wasn't unknown for muntjac to wander in, there being a small herd of the animals in the local park. Jeff and Anya sat in a pair of Adirondack chairs on her terrace, Anya pulling up a rug that had been on her chair up over her knees. The combination of cigarette, beer and the night-time stillness made Jeff even more relaxed and for a few minutes neither of them spoke. He knew, however, that

that wasn't the plan, so he wasn't surprised when Anya broke the silence.

"So, Jeffrey, are you going to tell me what's going on?"

Jeff took a drag on his cigarette and watched the plume of smoke as he exhaled. Where to start, he wondered.

"Anya, I don't know, really. I've been taking my meds, I'm sure I have. It's just... I started seeing things and..."

"What things? Tell me about it."

Jeff related the incident with the pale woman in the bookshop, and then the theatre. After more prompting, he sketched, briefly, the outline of what he'd seen afterwards, before waking up in the hospital. What he could remember of it, at least. For the most part, Anya just let him talk and he realised that he'd been needing to do this since he came back around. To get it out of his system, hear it out loud and realise the absurdity of what he'd seen, the outlandish nature of his psychosis. Once he'd finished, he felt better equipped to start putting it behind him.

"And you think it was just tiredness, darling? You have been working awfully hard since... Since Ciara left."

Jeff ignored the reference to his ex. "I guess work's been so busy, I've neglected to take any time off, just let myself be swept along by it. I don't really have much to do when I'm not at work. I'm not seeing anyone at the moment, the flat feels so empty."

"You can always move back in here, you know that."

Jeff looked over at his stepmother, grateful for the love he could see in her offer. "I love you, Anya, but I don't think we make good housemates. We've come a long way to reach where we are now and, honestly, I don't think I could bear to lose that."

She smiled at him, a tear in one eye, and reached out a thin, bony hand to him, which he took hold of and squeezed.

"Your father would be proud of you."

"He'd be proud of us. All of us." Jeff stubbed out his cigarette, half smoked. He didn't enjoy the taste anywhere near as much as he remembered. "I'm going to stay with Anoush for a while. Phil's gone again…"

"That fucker! Again? Why hasn't she told me?"

Jeff dropped Anya's hand and took another swig of beer. "You know Anoush, much happier running other people's lives than sorting her own shit out."

Anya let out a throaty laugh, startling a fox that bolted, previously unseen, out of the hedge a few feet away and down to the trees at the bottom of the garden.

Jeff finished the dregs of his beer. "I'm getting tired, Anya, I think I need to go home." He stood up. "You coming in?"

Anya stretched out her legs, adjusted the blanket and took out her cigarettes. "I think I'm going to sit here for a bit. Put the guard in front of the fire and tell my daughter I said goodbye."

Jeff rested his hand on her shoulder and gave it a gentle squeeze. "Don't fall asleep out here."

She put her hand up and patted his. "Don't worry, darling, one more cigarette, I swear."

He left her and went inside.

It was Saturday and Anoush had left Jeff alone for the afternoon. Shopping probably, but Jeff had slept in and only found a hurried note on the table when he finally awoke, with no clues as to her whereabouts, just a vague indication of when he could expect her back and an instruction to eat.

Jeff once again cursed Phil for taking his games console with him when he left, settling instead for messing up the absentee husband's Netflix algorithm with an extended *Friends* marathon. Too late for breakfast, he made himself some toast, leaving the jar of peanut butter on the coffee table for top-ups.

Dozing on and off for a while, Jeff decided in the afternoon, after a ten-minute walk around the block, to find a live stream of the Norwich City match. Not his home team, but Jeff didn't particularly like football anyway, so it entertained him during football conversations with his colleagues to only talk about a team no one else remotely cared about.

A wet and miserable afternoon at Carrow Road suited Jeff's mood. He was out of sorts; as much as he didn't want to admit it even to himself, he wished Anoush was here so they could hang out. Thinking about Anoush reminded him about his meds, so he rooted around in his satchel and found them, knocking them back with a big gulp of pink squash.

The match, predictably, wasn't offering much drama and Jeff lay on his side on the couch, half listening to the match and half wondering whether he was hungry enough to get another round of toast. The commentary was white noise in his ears, and he was almost asleep again when one of the voices broke through the fog.

"... Well this isn't what you think it is..."

Jeff sat bolt upright. The voice hadn't been female, it was the same Norfolk accent droning on, but the use of that phrase... He started at the livestream, wondering if it was just coincidence, but a panning shot of the crowd seemed to linger for a moment, amongst the sea of yellow and green, on a slender, pale figure...

Jeff slammed the laptop screen down. Chest heaving, what felt like cold fingers seemed to clutch his heart. He took another gulp of squash, then stood up and paced the room. A candle caught his eye on the bookshelf, in front of a selection of books on meditation. No doubt that would be Anoush's answer.

Checking again he had his keys on him, he pulled the door closed behind him and took the emergency packet of cigarettes out of his pocket. He leant back against the door and lit one, apologising to the old lady who arrived and tried to enter the building, stepping to one side to let her pass as she muttered something under her breath. Stepping out onto the pavement, glancing up and down the street for the pale young woman, he bundled his hands in his jacket pockets and headed down to the café at the end of the street. He needed strong, sweet tea, and the anonymous presence of others.

The cafe was moderately busy, thank goodness. Checking first for any sign of the pale apparition, Jeff got himself a cup of tea and a sausage roll and found himself a seat by the window. Looking out onto the street, he added three spoons of sugar to his mug and took a first sip. Hot and sweet, exactly what he wanted.

It was an overcast October day, but dry and relatively warm, and the sun was fighting its way through a few gaps in the cloud. Grim, but prospects of change in the near future. A good omen? Jeff wasn't sure. He took out his phone, signed into the café's wifi and kept half an eye on the football scores as he made his way through the sausage roll. Pastry crumbs in his beard and on his pullover, Jeff was now oblivious to the rest of the people in the café, his attention fixed on the street outside.

"Is this seat taken?"

Jeff started, looking up to see a young woman with a blonde bob standing over him, mug and plate in hand, gesturing with her sandwich at the seat across the table from him. His heart raced and he could do little more than nod, before remembering what nodding meant and shaking his head.

"No... I mean, it's fine, it's free."

The woman smiled at him and sat down. She was slightly younger than him, late twenties he guessed. Nice eyes, a striking green, and an amused smile... her face. He could see her face. There was no ambiguity, that was her face, right there. He exhaled in relief, catching her attention and she looked up at him.

"Are you okay?"

"No, yeah, I'm..." Jeff composed himself. "I'm sorry, long day, overslept, bit out of it. Came out to wake myself up a bit. Sorry." He took another mouthful of tea, then picked up his phone and started scrolling, aimlessly, but with the intention of passing himself off as vaguely normal. He winced internally as he sensed the woman's amusement at his discomfort.

"I'm Sal."

He looked up. "Jeff."

"Thanks for letting me share your table, Jeff." She was still smiling as she took a book out of her shoulder bag and started reading. Jeff let himself relax a bit. Come on, it's fine. Normal. Normal woman. Normal café. Get a grip, son.

The woman, Sal, was soon engrossed in her book, and was seemingly oblivious to the occasional glance Jeff shot her across the table. Norwich were grinding their way towards what looked like a nil-nil draw, no doubt with the intention of ballsing it up in the last five minutes. Jeff wished he'd brought a book too. He settled for scrolling through Facebook.

After the match drew to a close, Jeff realised he was still hungry and got up, deliberating over whether to get some cake or head back to Anoush's and order a pizza. Anoush might even be home by now, he realised. Some Carcassonne and a movie might shift the day's mood a bit, but then this made him realise that if he got home and Anoush wasn't back, the unease he'd felt all day might start to grow again.

The time it was taking to work through this thought process meant that he had now been stood up longer than the decision to order something else necessitated, and Sal was looking up at him again.

"You off, Jeff?"

Jeff froze. What to say, what to say?

"I … No. I'm getting another tea. Do you want anything?"

Well shit, that won't seem weird.

"That's a kind offer, Jeff. Yes, I would. I'll have another latte."

"Muffin?"

"Excuse me?"

Shit, shit shit.

"A cake, sorry, do you want a cake with your coffee…" Jeff was growing increasingly flustered, much to Sal's evident amusement.

"I wouldn't say no to a piece of that caramel shortbread."

"Right. Right."

A brief moment's pause, then Jeff turned around and went up to the counter.

He stood there, staring fixedly at the menu on the wall behind the counter while the beardy, aproned hipster put his order together and was able to just about get his head back in the game by the time he was presented with his drinks and cakes. Girding his loins, he returned to the table. Sal carefully bent the corner of her page over (what the hell?) and placed her book down.

"That's very decent of you, Jeff. How much…"

Jeff waved his hand. "No bother."

Sal, for the first time, suddenly seemed slightly uncomfortable herself, then seemed to put her caution aside. "Well, thank you."

Jeff took a sip of tea, and a bite of his blueberry muffin. He'd wanted a chocolate muffin, but an inexplicable desire to look more grown-up had prompted him to go for what he thought was a slightly healthier, and therefore the more mature, option. Sal took a bit of her shortbread, raising her other hand up under her chin to catch the tiny shower of crumbs that inevitably fell. She nodded, her eyes widening slightly.

"Mmm, good…"

"Yeah? Good."

Putting her cake down again, she daintily wiped her mouth with a napkin.

"So, Jeff. Do you regularly come to cafes to pick up women?" She was grinning.

"Hey, I was sat here first. You came over to me, remember?"

"There was nowhere else to sit."

"Fine, of course, but I didn't sit down next to you, is all I'm saying."

"I'm kidding, Jeff."

"I know." Another sip of tea. "Good book?"

Sal did what everyone did when asked about the book they're reading, she picked it up and read the back cover to herself again as she answered, "Yeah, it's okay. Pretty good actually. Not my usual sort of thing. A friend lent it to me."

"What is your usual sort of thing?"

"I'm more of a sci-fi fan, if I'm honest."

The chat went on, as chat does. Jeff loosened up a bit, Sal continued to look wryly amused by him, but it was nice. Simple. When she'd finished her coffee and shortbread, she stood up to leave. She didn't offer her number; Jeff didn't ask for it. It wasn't often, Jeff thought to himself, that such interactions occurred without any agenda behind them. He could have felt disappointed, but frankly it was more refreshing than anything. Outside, Sal looked back in through the window and gave him a wave. He offered an embarrassing two-finger-tap-on-his-forehead-style salute, cringed internally and gave her enough time to skedaddle before getting up himself. She'd headed in the direction of Anoush's flat, so best give her time to not think she was being followed. Which she wasn't.

Anoush was home when he got back, and he could tell she had been disconcerted to find him absent, so Jeff was impressed at the fact that there were no messages or texts on his phone. Clearly, she was fighting to give him space. But the relief on her face was palpable when he walked in and the hug she gave him was more than perfunctory.

"Pizza tonight, babes?"

Cutting her some slack for the slack she'd cut him, he swallowed down his distaste for his own half-sister calling him 'babes' and just said, "Sure. Want me to order?"

She was leaning against the kitchen counter, phone in hand. "No, it's fine, I'm on the app now. Usual?"

"Of course."

"Extras? Drinks?"

Jeff opened the fridge to check the state of their no/low supply. All good. "No drink, maybe some garlic dippers?"

"Done." Anoush hit 'send' with a flourish and popped her phone in her back pocket, gave Jeff a peck on the cheek and went to the sofa, picking up the remote as she flopped down. Clearly there was no boardgame on the cards for tonight, Jeff realised as he remembered it was Saturday. No doubt they'd spend the evening watching terrible talent shows before arguing over what movie to watch. His afternoon with Sal, after the initial discomfort, had been pleasant enough that he decided to forego the usual pantomime of complaints at his sister's taste in televisual entertainment. Heck, he might even let her pick the film later.

The pizza was due to take half an hour, which therefore meant probably forty minutes or so. Jeff decided to take a shower. Stood there, shampooing his beard, the room steaming up and water streaming down his face, he felt the final remnants of his earlier disquiet flow out of him. He could almost see the dark thoughts circling the plughole before disappearing. He took a few minutes longer than normal, just stood there in the hot stream, rolling his neck and rotating his shoulders. God bless Anoush and her insistence on installing a proper rain shower. Phil had seemed happy to live with just a bath and one of those rubber shower attachments you slipped onto the taps like some kind of student.

Towelling himself off, Jeff started to feel hungry, and by the time he'd thrown on his jeans and a fresh t-shirt, he was delighted to hear the doorbell sound. "I'll go!" he yelled. Anoush was no doubt engrossed in something, and he was in a good mood.

He buzzed the delivery guy in, waited a few moments by the door and then opened it at the knock. He looked out into the hall to see a slim figure in a red fleece holding an ungainly delivery bag. A girl, he realised, though her head was facing down, and her face was masked by the peak of her cap, from under which poked light blonde hair.

She lifted the bag and reached inside, pulling out a couple of boxes and handing them to Jeff. He took hold but the girl didn't let go. There was, he realised, an odd smell in the hallway. Sort of oily.

"O… kay…"

The girl mumbled something, then coughed, a deep hacking cough. Don't tell me Anoush didn't pay, he thought.

"Sorry?" He looked down at the pizza box. The girl's hands were very pale, he realised.

"I said, this isn't what you think it is."

The girl looked up, and Jeff realised it was the light in the hallway that made her almost-white hair look blonde…

5

Was that fireworks? Bit bloody early, it was still October... the bed didn't feel right. This wasn't Anoush's flat... Anoush, the name suddenly felt the wrong shape in his mind. The fireworks, the scratchy sheets, fuck... Jeff sprung up... The room he was in was small, oppressively claustrophobically so, and plaster was crumbling off the walls. There was snow on the windowsill and something smelled foul. Jeff swung his legs off the low bed, almost knocking over a bucket that stood on the floor, and coughed up a mouthful of gloopy, acrid phlegm. The bucket was the source of the smell. Some of it at least, Jezz realised. Was that piss on his sheets?

An explosion rocked the building, sending a thin shower of dust cascading from the ceiling. Not fireworks, he knew. It was a bombardment. Where the hell *was* he?

Jezz staggered to the door, nearly falling as he flung it open. "Nora!" he shouted. He stepped out onto the landing, oblivious to the fact that he was dressed only in his vest top and long johns. "Nora!"

"Fuck's sake, Jezz." Teemu appeared from the door to the next room, rubbing his eyes. It obviously took him a moment to work out what was going because he stared at Jezz, before shouting down the stairwell: "Price! Jezz is up!"

The captain's face appeared from a doorway further down the corridor. "What do you mean?"

"I mean he's up! He's Jezz!"

Jezz looked at Teemu in a bewildered state. "Where are we? What's going on? What do you mean, I'm Jezz? Who else…?"

Teemu put his arm round Jezz and was about to guide him back into his room, when he got a whiff of the smell inside. "Oh shit, Jezz. Come on." He reached in and grabbed Jezz's boots and jacket. Jezz, still dazed, took the boots he was given and put them on, not bothering to fasten them. Teemu helped him on with his jacket, then escorted him down the stairs.

They descended two floors and out through the front door. There was snow on the ground, of course, and a chill wind startled Jezz, clearing some of the fog in his mind. He stood shivering in his long johns. Teemu took a cursory look up and down the street before hustling Jezz across to the building opposite. "They've still got running water here, buddy. We need to get you hosed down."

The building had been a hotel in a past existence. A tired looking major stood behind the front desk arguing with a belligerent man in a United Korean Militia uniform.

"Major Dempsey? Our man's back up, can I get him showered?"

Dempsey didn't even look up, just waved Teemu through. The two of them headed down a corridor then took a flight of stairs one floor up. There, a bustle of activity met them, as a flurry of officers were scurrying in and out of the hotel ballroom, delivering and collecting reports. Teemu, still supporting Jezz, waited a moment for a break in the traffic, then pushed Jezz on and around to the next staircase. Up this flight, and they were met by a sergeant, who pointed them down a corridor towards a short queue of soldiers waiting by the entrance to one of the hotel rooms.

Teemu, outranking most of them, walked straight past them to the head of the queue, ignoring their groans and complaints. One man, bare-chested with his towel over his shoulder and a toothbrush in his mouth looked like he was going to try and stand in their way, but Teemu, not even waiting for the inevitable show of bravado, reached a hand out, took a grasp of the man's forehead and smacked the man's head back against the wall. "I've got a wounded lieutenant here who's just woken up from a coma covered in his own piss and shit, now *fuck off*."

He didn't stop to see how the man would react, just barged past and into the room. Inside, a thin, wiry young man was towelling himself dry. He didn't look up as Teemu and Jezz barged in. "I'm nearly done." For a moment Jezz thought Teemu was going to grab him and throw him out on the landing, but Teemu just helped Jezz through to the bathroom.

"You okay to do this yourself?"

Jezz just looked at him, not wanting to admit out loud that he didn't think he was. Teemu's voice, deep but soft, was comforting as he patted Jezz on the cheek. "Okay buddy, just sit there a minute."

Jezz perched on the toilet as Teemu stepped back into the main room. The young man was pulling on his uniform now, seemingly indifferent to the interruption. Teemu leant against the bathroom door frame, watching the man finish up and grab his pack. Then, as the man left, Teemu stepped into the corridor behind him, gave the queue of men fixed stare and pulled the door shut, locking it as he did so.

He came back into the bathroom. Jezz looked up at him, his eyes moist and full of confusion.

"What's going on, Teemu?"

"We arrived Ziyang a couple of days ago. You've been out of it since you nearly gunned down a group of refugees leaving Chongqing on foot. We thought Price was going to insist we hand you over to the first med team we passed, but he let Nora tend to you in the cabin. He saw you right," Teemu's voice was tinged with something Jezz couldn't place, but it was clear the big man had been taken aback by their commander's loyalty. "He may be a prick, but he saw you right. Nora kept you dosed up and as clean as she could while we drove here. Luckily, we didn't encounter any bugs the whole way. When we arrived, we tracked down the rest of the division. Unfortunately, the Eltiy'ch had found them first. Ziyang's a total clusterfuck, man." Teemu was perched on the side of the bath now and as he said this, he leaned over and started running the taps. "The north and the east of the city are overrun with enemy forces. We might not have seen them, but they were on their way. Colonel Holt and the rest… There's no way they got out, man." He paused. "There's Korean militia here, Indians, even some European detachments. Chinese, of course. But it's street-to-street stuff. The bombardments don't stop, and they seem to have infinite bodies to throw at us. Sichuan province is fucked, man. We can't get out of here soon enough."

Teemu tested the water, then as it carried on filling the bath, stood up and reached out to Jezz. Jezz lifted his arms and let the big man remove his jacket, then his top. He didn't say anything as Teemu pulled him to his feet, or as he lifted first one foot, and then the other, to remove his boots. His hands on Teemu's shoulders, he stepped out of his long johns and stood there naked in the steaming bathroom. Teemu turned the taps off and then gently helped the frightened and still bewildered Jezz into the tub.

"I haven't done this since my kid started school." Teemu reached for a sponge and started to soap it up.

It wasn't just the piss and the vomit (Teemu had, fortunately, exaggerated the shit, much as he had the 'coma'). It was the entire dirt and grime and oil of the whole failed Chongqing offensive. Jezz hadn't had anything more than a hooker's bath for weeks and as he stood in the hotel room towelling off, he looked at himself in the mirror grimacing at what he saw. Thin, almost emaciated. The wound on his arm was still raw, although Nora had clearly done an astounding job of keeping infection out. There was another, older scar on his forehead. As he slicked his wet hair back, he was alarmed to see it had started to thin out since the last time he'd paid it any attention. Whenever that was. His beard was patchy and bedraggled, nothing new there, but now it was starting to go white. All in all, he painted a dismal picture. A shadow of the man who'd flown into Myitkyina a year ago. He wiped the back of his hand aggressively across his cheeks to get rid of the tears, just as the door to the hotel room banged open.

"There he is. Officer in the room, man, put some fucking clothes on."

Teemu had disappeared a few minutes earlier. By that time, the queue outside had already been siphoned off to another room, the sergeant at the top of the stairs obviously briefed as to Jezz's situation. The Finn was back now, following Price and Nora into the room. It was Price who'd hailed him. Jezz turned to the crew and almost started sobbing, but Price, though it transpired not as heartless as they'd all assumed, was only willing to go so far. He picked Jezz's top up from the bed and threw it at him. "You need to eat, get a move on."

"Can I…?" Jezz gestured at the towel around his waist and the long johns on the bed.

Nora, lighting a cigarette, tossed his trousers and a clean top onto the bed for him. "Grow a pair, buddy. It's not like I've never seen a tiny dick before." She threw herself onto the room's second bed, laid back with her arms behind her head. She kept the cigarette in her mouth as she blew a plume of smoke up around it like a mushroom cloud. She was wearing dark glasses, obviously picked up a from a black-market dealer in the city, and her hair was tied back with more care than Jezz had seen her show in weeks.

He dropped the towel and threw it at her, before reaching for his underwear and quickly getting dressed. Teemu had ducked into the bathroom and the other three winced, berating him as the sounds of a particularly hearty, earthy shit came through the door. "For fuck's sake, Teemu, you had to do that here?" Nora yelled.

Jezz, on the verge of tears again at the normality of the crew's badinage, masked his emotion by turning back to the mirror and running a comb back through his hair, dishevelled again by the putting on of his top. In the mirror, he saw Nora looking at him from the bed, her eyes just visible over the top of the dark glasses. They stayed like that for a moment, eyes locked. Then she tipped her head back and let out another thick belch of smoke.

"So, where the hell do we get something to eat in this shithole?" asked Jezz.

"Jue-meng's!" called out Teemu and Nora in unison, the big man arriving back in the main room, followed by an unhealthy miasma that stung in the back of Jezz's throat.

"Oh, fuck me, Teemu, we're supposed to be getting something to eat..."

Jue-meng's Noodle Palace was just a few blocks down from the hotel. Jezz, feeling reinvigorated from being clean and back in the lively company of the crew, realised he was famished. As Teemu helped him along the street behind Nora and Price, he was soon grinning with the rest of them.

Price had materialised a bottle of whisky from his pack. He refused to divulge its origins but passed it around his crew almost cheerfully. Between the war and being put in command, Price had been robbed of all the easy-going qualities Jezz had known in him from growing up, leaving just a near-constant anger, but he seemed genuinely relieved to have Jezz back and the group was in high spirits as they got to Jue-Meng's. The place was lively with combined forces personnel, but Jue-meng himself appeared as the group entered, waving and grinning.

"My favourite customers, come in, come in!" He addressed the group, but it was clear that it was Teemu's prodigious appetite that secured them their own booth, much to the disgruntlement of the Malay party that was turfed out to accommodate them. Staff cleared away the remains of the Malay's meal and in a cascade of broken Cantonese, Teemu ordered what sounded to Jezz like enough food for a dozen people.

That turned out to be not far wrong as the three waiters started to pile up their table with dishes, along with twelve bottles of local beer. Teemu and Nora set to upending one dish into another to make room on the table.

"How are we affording this?" asked Jezz to Price, beside him.

"Are you kidding? US dollars go a long way in this town, and we haven't spent anything for months. Besides," he added conspiratorially, leaning into Jezz as he did so, stale whisky on his breath, drops of spicy garlic sauce on the fringe of his moustache. "I had a few supplies stashed away in a safe house here from before Chongqing. Prices have gone up, and when I say 'up', I mean…" Price jabbed his finger skywards. Jezz had never seen Price like this, and he started to wonder exactly how long the captain had been drunk for.

Jue-meng hovered as more plates were delivered. He chatted in Cantonese to Teemu, oblivious to the fact that the big man, now piling into the food with a vengeance, couldn't understand spoken Cantonese anywhere near as much as he could speak it himself. Once or twice the bar owner tried to engage Nora, but she largely ignored him. Knocking back her second beer, every now and then she'd look at him and say, "I. Don't. Understand. Speak no Chinese." Nora's Cantonese was, so far as Jezz knew, fluent, but her disdain at being mistaken for a local meant she hardly ever admitted it.

Food delivered, Jezz and Price joined Teemu in setting to. For a while they were silent, though the bar certainly was not. Western music pumped out of the tinny radio set on the counter, in a bitter contest with the Chinese folk music that Jue-meng for some reason still had playing over the restaurant speakers. The place was full of lively chatter in a disparate spread of languages, mostly good natured, but the crew was intent on filling their bellies. It wasn't until Price leaned over, pointing to a plate in front of Nora and asked, "Are you eating that?" that any of them spoke.

Nora shook her head. She opened her third beer and lit another cigarette.

"You eating at all, Nora?" asked Jezz.

"Gimme a chance. You wolves are scaring me, Imma wait until it's safe to put my hands in there before I start." Her words were slightly slurred, and Jezz felt an icy shiver down his back. Soldiers drinking was to be expected, but he now got a real sense that his crew were masking a lot of unease with a lot of alcohol, and maybe had been for some time.

He leaned back in his seat. "I get one of those?"

"Sure," Nora reached over and offered him the pack. He drew one out, lit it, inhaled deeply then cricked his neck back to blow the smoke straight up. It tasted good. Between that and the beer, he was starting to feel a little buzz.

Price was slowing down now, picking at the dishes in reach rather than shovelling. Teemu looked up briefly to assess the others' progress, shrugged, put his head down and ploughed on.

"How long this time?"

Nobody needed to ask what Jezz was referring to.

"About a week, all in. You've been feverish, talking a lot of nonsense when you've been awake, but mainly sleeping." Price put his chopsticks down and picked up his beer. "We took you to a doc when we got in, but he sent us off with a flea in our ear. Actual injuries to deal with, he said."

"I should have knocked that fucker out cold," muttered Teemu, pausing in his gorging to wash it down with a little beer.

"Yeah, that would have helped," said Nora, elbowing the big man in the flesh where she assumed his ribs were. He shoved back, tetchily.

"Fuck sake, I'm eating."

"So is this going to keep happening?" Jezz picked nervously at the label on his beer bottle.

"Probably, I don't know. Maybe. Doc in Chongqing thought you got off pretty light, but the truth is I don't think anyone knows how the alien phero-munitions work. Not really. And certainly not long-term, obviously. Some people go nuts. On the other hand, some people experience one vision, are out for a few hours, then never seem to have any more problems. Body chemistry, weight, length of exposure, all of those could have an effect. Plus, we've no idea whether it's one standard chemical composition, or if there's a hundred different flavours. Nobody knows a fucking thing." Price stuffed a handful of prawn toast into his mouth, then elbowed Jezz to let him out of the booth. "Gotta hit the whizz palace."

Jezz shuffled out of the booth, let Price out and slipped back in. He leaned forward with his elbows on the table, taking another drag on his cigarette. He fixed Nora with a look. "You ought to eat something."

Nora shrugged, but she dropped her cigarette into an empty bottle and picked up her chopsticks, started poking around half-heartedly in a bowl of beef noodles.

"He's worried I'm going to be no use, isn't he."

Teemu scoffed. "Who gives a shit? The show's over, Jezz. We came to Ziyang to regroup, and all we found was more Eltiy'ch, more carnage and more chaos. Chongqing's gone, Sichuan's falling. Yunnan was evacuated two weeks ago. We're getting pushed back on every front. This is just a rest stop on the way to Xizang. Ain't none of us no fucking use to anyone. Gonna be in fucking India by the end of the year."

A group of Indian officers sat the booth opposite looked up, not hearing exactly what Teemu said but registering the mention of their homeland, and the tone used. Teemu waved a chicken leg at them. "No offence."

The officers muttered to themselves and carried on with their meal.

"We're just gonna tie you up, throw you in the trunk and get the fuck outta Dodge."

Jezz gave him the finger, but his heart wasn't in it. None of them had expected Ziyang to be the kick-off for a counter-offensive, but it sounded like all of China was about to go Fubar.

Price lurched back to the table. "We done? I need some fresh air."

"You okay, chief?"

Price pointed over his shoulder. "Just threw up."

Teemu's shoulders shook with laughter and even Nora grinned. The group extricated themselves from the booth and staggered to the door, Nora grabbing the last three bottles of beer on the table as they did so. Throwing down a wad of notes, Price gave Jue-meng a vague approximation of a salute, before Teemu picked the diminutive bar owner up in a huge bear hug. Jue-meng grinned, but the grin had a glassy, fixed quality to it, Jezz noticed. Our money may be good, he thought, but we're still the foreign assholes.

The crew wandered the busy streets for a few hours, stopping in bars just long enough to get more supplies. There was no plan discussed aloud, just an unspoken consensus that they were too restless to lay in anywhere for the night. Much of Ziyang felt the same way, it seemed.

By two in the morning, they found themselves walking along the Tuo River. Shops and bars were still open, and a host of boats were making their way up and down the waterway, military and civilian. The sounds of bombardment could still be heard over to the east, but tonight it was mixed with actual fireworks being set off, as if it was some kind of public holiday. From every bar and restaurant, a never-ending stream of soldiers poured in and out. Street vendors yelled out over the sound of a hundred different songs being blasted through tinny speakers, trying to entice passers-by to buy what meagre scraps they still had to sell. The occasional jeep or truck wove its way slowly through the crowds on the street, but mostly people were on foot. Local women, dressed in their finest outfits, walked the streets trying to catch the eye of the less-drunk soldiers, hoping to make enough money to buy their way away from the front; to book one of the rapidly shrinking number of flights out before the only option left was to walk. The successful ones didn't bother to take their catches far, and doorways were used as impromptu bedrooms. Ziyang was alive and had no intention of going to sleep, because at any moment the long sleep might come, the one there was no waking up from.

Jezz stared around at the chaotic streets, marvelling at what felt like a party atmosphere, with a barely detectable undercurrent of terror. Chinese faces stared down at the carnival-like scenes from many of the windows, some cheering, some throwing fireworks. Some just looking, expressionless, at their city dying, knowing that they would soon be next, already having given up any idea of escape. An old man, wild strands of white hair that barely outnumbered the minimal number of teeth in his mouth, bumped into Jezz and grabbed his jacket with one hand. The old man's other hand held firmly onto the wrist of a small girl, no more than ten years of age. He started to chatter something at Jezz, far too fast for comprehension, his face trying to exude warmth and encouragement even as tears rolled down his cheeks. Nora stepped in and pushed the old man away, shouting at him in her rarely-used Cantonese. The old man stumbled as he was pushed back and fell onto his backside on the pavement. Jezz went to help him up, but Nora stopped him. She cursed the old man and dragged Jezz away. Jezz realised he didn't want to know what the old man was offering.

Teemu was so drunk now he could barely talk, just staggering along with a bottle of vodka he'd bought from a Scandinavian press team they'd run into. Price was doing his best to corral him into something approaching a straight line but was spending as much time placating the various groups of soldiers Teemu barged into. The big man came to a sudden halt in the middle of the road, swaying gently, his head thrown back, looking at the stars.

A group of Korean soldiers stood on the pavement staring at him. A couple were laughing, but most of them looked at Teemu with icy contempt. One of them spat on the pavement.

Jezz would have put good money on Teemu not having a clue what was going on, that he didn't even know where he was. But the moment the Korean spat, Teemu spun around and threw the bottle of vodka at the group. It missed the spitter but smacked into the head of one of his comrades. The soldier went over like a felled tree. The Koreans started yelling. A few of them stepped out into the road, but the initiative was with Teemu. With a roar, he lunged at the group. At the sight of this ferocious, bearded Viking coming full tilt at them, the Koreans spooked. They turned and ran. Teemu lumbered to a stop after only a few steps. The entire street was now watching him, swaying precariously right over the crumpled figure of the unconscious Korean on the pavement.

"Fuck sake, Teemu…" Nora screeched. Price ran over to the big man, just in time to utterly fail to stop him toppling forward and lying face-down in the gutter, blood trickling from his jaw.

Jezz couldn't help himself. As Nora continued to curse, as Price started to pull at the unconscious driver's arm, trying to roll him up onto the pavement, Jezz crouched down, falling onto his arse, shaking with laughter. He laid back on the road, howling. The Eltiy'ch, the retreat, the fall of Chongqing, the drink, Teemu… It was all too much for Jezz's fractured state of mind. Jezz laughed until he wept.

Price stopped a jeep from their battalion that was passing and with the help of the jeep's driver and his mate, managed to load the bearded drunk onto it. Teemu was now snoring loud enough to wake the dead. Price directed the jeep back to their digs, after Jezz and Nora politely declined the invitation to help him put Teemu to bed. "Besides," Jezz added, "my room's awash with vomit and piss, so excuse me if I find somewhere else to kip down tonight."

The jeep roared off, Price holding onto Teemu with one hand and giving the finger back to his unhelpful crew with the other. Jezz returned the gesture, then took a long pull from his beer. The bottle was empty, so he dropped it where he stood, bundled his arms into his jacket and started to trudge off down the road. Nora skipped up to him, put her arm through his and together they left as the watching crowd lost interest and returned to their own distractions.

They wandered the riverside for what seemed like hours, hardly talking. Nora was leaning on his shoulder now as they walked and Jezz was starting to become conscious of how nice that felt. Price would have had a fit, and rightly so, seeing two of his crew looking as if they were fraternising. Or maybe he wouldn't, not now. This all had an air of finality to it, somehow. Like none of the former rules applied. And as it turned out, Jezz wasn't wrong.

They stopped by another stretch of street food vendors arrayed along the quayside and bought pancakes from a woman who looked to Jezz as if she was at least a hundred years old. Stood right on the quayside, Jezz watched the boats pass as he stood with one foot up on the railings. Nora, next to him, leant against the barrier, her back to the river. She finished her pancake first, wiping her hands on her trousers and then tucking her now somewhat dishevelled hair behind her ears.

"I'm leaving, Jezz."

He turned sharply to face her. "You're what?"

It wasn't impossible. They, like most of the troops in Sichuan, were volunteers, not conscripts. Ordinary people who'd flown over to join the fight against the Eltiy'ch, this threat to all of humanity that was laying waste to China. Nobody could stop Nora flying home again. But he was shocked, nevertheless.

"I've made up my mind. There's a plane to Frankfurt tonight, taking press home. I've bought myself a seat on it."

Jezz stared at her, but she didn't return his gaze, kept her eyes firmly on the pavement. They both stayed like that for a moment, then Jezz took out another cigarette, lit it, and turned back to look out over the river. "Well, shit."

"I'm sorry…" Nora started to say, as she turned around to face the river too.

"You shouldn't be. If the rest of us had any fucking sense we'd be on that flight with you."

There was the merest hint of dawn now. Jezz, his eyes darting sideways momentarily, could see Nora's profile. She wasn't crying. Didn't look remorseful, even, just resolute. Her mind was made up, he could tell straight away. And even if it wasn't, there's not the smallest part of him that would try to talk her out of it.

"You don't think I'm abandoning you?"

"Go home, Nora. See your family. Be with your mother. This war's done."

She nodded. She was shivering slightly now, they both were. He moved over to step behind her, enveloping her in his arms from behind. He rested his chin on her shoulder, feeling the closeness of her face beside his, and they stood there for a while, looking out over the water.

Something changed. He couldn't quite tell when he had stopped reassuring a friend, and when he had started feeling conscious of her ass pressed up against his crotch. But he was now painfully aware of his body reacting to the closeness and so, it seemed, was Nora. She shifted slightly on her feet, fixing her hands on his to stop him moving away as she coyly swayed her hips slightly, encouraging his dick to swell further.

Then she pushed him away. He was about to apologise, but she put a finger to his lips. Taking hold of his wrist, she pulled him towards one of the alleys that led away from the quay. Jezz looked around but needn't have bothered. The whole city was drunk, and the Chinese had long stopped giving a shit what the foreign soldiers overrunning their country got up to. In the alleyway, Nora pushed Jezz up against the wall and kissed him, hard, her wet tongue forcing its way into his mouth. The kiss was rough, angry almost, and Jezz started as she slipped a hand down between them and, with a deftness that defied belief, unfastened his trousers and shot inside to grab at him. With her hand grasping him firmly, she spun the pair of them around, so her back was now to the wall, then turned again so that Jezz was behind her. With one arm steadying herself on the building, and one hand behind her back, still holding onto his swollen cock, Nora lowered her head and muttered something that sounded like 'Fuck me'.

Jezz's breathing tightened as he reached down and unfastened her trousers. He grabbed the waistbands of her trousers and underwear together and slid them just far enough down her thighs that he could feel her naked ass against him.

She leaned forward and, bending his knees just enough, Jezz pushed between her legs, hearing her moan, "Fuuuck," as he slipped inside her. For a moment, they were still, both savouring the feel of his engorged cock filling her pussy. Then, to the sound of a city in chaos, distant shellfire exploding, lit only by the moon and a constant barrage of fireworks, and before the smell of the alley could kill the moment, Jezz started to move his hips…

They broke apart with a casual air neither of them felt, as they pretended to not be doing up their trousers.

"If I'm pregnant, I'm gonna come back and shoot you myself."

"If you're pregnant, I promise you won't have to."

She punched him on the arm. "You got a cigarette?"

"Sure."

He lit two, and passed one to Nora as they stepped out of the alley and back out onto the quay. Nobody seemed to pay them the slightest attention. They moved off down the quay, watched only by the old pancake vendor.

Jezz had forgotten the state of his room and recoiled in disgust when he went to enter it, after Nora had guided him back to the building. She winked at him as she left him stood by the door, waltzing down the corridor to her own quarters.

"Can't I...?"

"Are you kidding? If Price saw you coming out of my room tomorrow, he'd shit. You're on your own now, kiddo." She blew him a kiss and disappeared around the corner.

From the room next door, Jezz could hear the roar of Teemu's snoring. Not even an option, he thought. Instead, he sighed and headed down to the street again. He wasn't that tired anyway, not for the moment, but he was hungry again.

He stepped out onto the pavement, trying to get his bearings. The sun was up now, but it was still early. The sound of distant bombardment sounded further away than ever, though Jezz wasn't naïve enough to think that it was because they were having any luck pushing the enemy back. It was classic erratic behaviour by the Eltiy'ch, the bombardments almost coming in pulses, heavy for a few hours, then light, heavy, light, as if the glacial heartbeat of their alien war machine.

Nowhere on the street seemed open, so Jezz picked a direction at random and started to stroll, fishing his last cigarette out of his pocket as he did so. A few hundred yards down the street he found an open minimart. Steeling himself against the strange, acrid odour within, he entered for supplies.

Picking up snacks here and there, he wasn't paying

much attention when he bumped into an old woman pushing a cart. Looking up, he started to apologise, but the words went unsaid as over the woman's shoulder, just disappearing around the top of the aisle, Jezz saw a slender, pale figure with short, almost white hair. His jaw dropped; cigarette stuck to his bottom lip. He didn't notice as one of the bags of rice-cakes in his hands slipped out of his grasp and onto the floor. Shoving the rest of his choices randomly back onto the shelf in front of him, he reached up and took the cigarette out of his mouth, then slowly backed down the aisle. The old Chinese woman he'd bumped into stared at the bizarre behaviour of the western soldier.

Jezz, at the end of the aisle, sidestepped into the next, in the direction the figure had passed. There, at the far end, dressed in fatigues and combat boots, was a young, pale woman with a shock of short, platinum blonde hair. She was looking at something on the shelf, but at the sound of Jezz's sharp intake of breath, she started to look up…

Jezz, heart pounding, fled out onto the street. Notnownotnownotnow… He looked up and down the street for… he didn't know what. Shelter? Company? Nora? There was a noise behind him, but he had no intention of turning round. Instead, he fled back in the direction of his digs.

At the front door to the building they were billeted in, he risked a glance over his shoulder. Behind him, in the middle of the street, just far enough away to render her features indistinct, stood the pale woman. Jezz bit down a scream and, making a split-second decision, instead of entering the building, started to pound down the street away from the figure haunting him. He reached round to the back of his waistband as he ran, instinctively grasping for a weapon that wasn't there.

He darted down a side street, then made a series of turns, soon becoming lost in the unfamiliar city. But every time he risked a glance behind him, she was there. Somehow always standing, not running as he was, but never further away.

"Hey!" came the indignant cry of a soldier that the fleeing Jezz nearly floored as he rounded the corner the man was stood on. "What the fuck, man?"

Jezz ignored him, stumbling on and ducking suddenly into a dive-bar that had opened early, or else hadn't shut at all. He backed into the bar, his gaze locked onto the door, waiting for the woman to appear. The bartender, half asleep on a stool by the bar, looked up. "What you want, soldier?" Other than that, the occupants of the bar, a handful of Chinese civilians and a couple of Korean soldiers, paid him no mind. Jezz backed away further from the door.

"The pisser, where's your pisser?"

The bartender pointed to the rear of the bar. "Customer only."

Jezz pulled a handful of notes from his pocket and dropped one on the bar. "Then get me a fucking beer. I need a piss."

Still the woman hadn't appeared and Jezz flung open the door of Ziyang's skankiest bathroom. He retreated into a cubicle, locked the door and sat on the bowl, breathing ragged.

The door to the bathroom slowly opened. There were footsteps. They stopped outside his cubicle and Jezz, frozen to the spot, not even breathing, felt his mind curl in on itself. The stench of stale piss seemed to mutate, taking on an acrid, oily taint. There was a hacking cough, and Jezz winced at the sound of a heavy glob of phlegm hitting the bathroom floor. The graffiti on the cubicle started to blur as a voice, low and feminine, spoke.

"Jezz, you need to stop running from me…"

6

Jezz woke up and sat bolt upright, coughing. Instinctively bringing his hand to his mouth, he felt the thick, viscous liquid seeping out of his mouth and through his fingers. Looking down in disgust, he wiped his hand over the bedspread. The liquid felt like honey.

This wasn't his bed, he realised straight away. The second thing he noticed was the silence. The Eltiy'ch bombardments had ceased completely. The third thing he noticed was that the sheets, and whatever he was wearing, again unfamiliar, were soaked with sweat.

He swung his legs out over the side of the bed and sat there for a few minutes to get his bearings. There was a table next to the bed, with a lamp on. Switching it on, he looked around at the room. Well, that's not right. The room was clean, orderly, spacious, if somewhat institutional. No damage, no signs of … anything. The glass in the window was intact, though that appeared to be reinforced, so maybe that explained that.

At the side of his bed, just where his feet were dangling, Jezz saw a pair of slippers. Slippers? Where the hell *am I*? But he slid his feet into them and stood up. Wavering slightly, on legs that felt underused, he made his way to the window. It was nighttime, he could see he was on the ground floor, there were trees, parkland…? There was a low building in view a few hundred feet away, one light on in the darkness.

"Toto, I've a feeling we're not in Kansas anymore," he muttered to himself. Wherever this was, it wasn't Ziyang. Had he been flown home? Had Anoush got him on the plane?

Jezz shook his head wildly. Anoush?? Who… Nora. Had Nora got him on the plane? Who the hell was Anoush? An image flashed in his mind of a young blonde woman. He involuntarily shuddered, but the pinched features of the woman in his mind weren't… He shook his head again.

He slowly, tentatively, walked over to the door and opened it onto a clean, white corridor. The idea that he was in a medical facility dawned on him. Maybe there was a doctor or a nurse who could tell him where he was. He padded softly towards a light streaming out of a room at the far end.

It was some kind of dayroom. An array of chairs, a sofa, boardgames and jigsaws haphazardly stacked on the shelves of an open cupboard, an old tv. Jezz frowned at the unfamiliar newsreader on the screen, but the volume was too low to fully register what they were talking about.

There was a chill breeze coming through the crack of an open door. Outside, Jezz could make out the figure, their back to him. Male, wearing white. A nurse then? The figure brought an arm up to their face and a moment later Jezz caught a whiff of tobacco. Cigarettes *and* answers? He lurched with almost indecent pace towards the door.

"Oh, hey man, you're up!" The man turned at the noise, flicked his cigarette butt out into the darkness and stepped inside, pulling the door to behind him. Dammit. Jezz halted and, suddenly light-headed, almost fell over.

"Hey hey hey, easy, man." The nurse, the uniform was unambiguous, rushed to Jezz and caught him, guided him down onto the nearest chair. "Take it easy, bro. You've been out of it for a while."

Jezz allowed the nurse to minister to him, too wiped out to argue or even speak for a minute or so.

"You want a drink, something to eat? You're probably starving. I've got some sandwiches in the fridge. Jeff, right?"

"Jezz," Jezz croaked. His throat was dry, he realised, and it felt like he hadn't spoken for a while.

"Okay, Jezz, cool. Sit tight, Jezz, Imma get you a drink and sandwich."

Jezz nodded, but by the time the nurse returned, he was asleep.

Doctor Singh sat cross-legged in his chair and gave Jeff a concerned look. "You told Jason your name was Jezz."

Jeff, slumped in the chair opposite, still in his pyjamas, gave a shrug. "I don't know, I was very confused. Didn't know where I was."

Doctor Singh made a note in the book he cradled on his lap. "It's not a nickname you go by, among a certain group of friends or anything?"

"No, no. I never… No. But it felt…"

"Go on."

"It felt like it was *my name*. I can't explain it. I didn't feel like me, I felt… other."

"Your identity in the psychosis, then. In this… future war?"

Jeff nodded. "Yeah. I mean, it's hazy. Even now I can remember less of it than I could an hour ago. But yeah, I think that's it. That's who I am… there."

There was a knock at the door. "Come," said Singh, not looking up.

Stella, his secretary came in. "Sorry to disturb you, Doctor Singh." She placed a familiar, comforting hand on Jeff's shoulder as she walked in. "You wanted the results of Jeffrey's bloods as soon as they came in."

"Thank you, Stella." Singh reached up and took the report she brandished at him. Patting Jeff again, she left the office, closing the door as softly as was humanly possible, as if to create the illusion of never having entered.

Singh took a minute or so to read and digest the report, then laid his pen on the notebook, closed it and put it on the table next to his chair. He removed his glasses and looked Jeff straight in the eye.

"All levels as expected. You were telling the truth about taking your meds."

Jeff, palms up, held out his hands in a gesture that spoke of relief that he was finally being believed. Singh templed his fingers under his chin.

"You've always been reluctant for me to increase the dose."

Jeff leaned back. It had been a sticking point in the past, but right now?

"You're the doctor."

Jeff sat outside at a picnic table. He was slumped forward, leaning on one arm. With the other, he was twisting a cigarette butt into an ashtray, grinding it over and over. Anoush was opposite him, lips pursed, swallowing down her criticisms of Jeff's smoking.

"Doctor Singh's putting my meds up."

"He told me."

"My bloods came back, nothing to suggest I wasn't missing them."

"He told me that too."

Jeff, still grinding the butt, raised his eyes to look at his half-sister. "Why do you sound so angry at me then?"

Anoush rolled her eyes. "I'm not angry, Jeff. I'm worried about you."

"Tell your face, then."

"Oh, sod off, Jeff. I want you to talk to me."

Jeff finally let go of the butt and languorously leant back, stretching. "About what?" He took another cigarette from the packet lying next to the ashtray.

"For goodness' sake," muttered Anoush under her breath. She snatched the packet from Jeff, took out a cigarette and then grabbed his lighter and lit it. Jeff stared at her.

"What? What now? What the hell?" Anoush gestured aimlessly with her cigarette. "We're all worried sick about you, Jeff, and you won't say anything to us about what you are going through. It's like you're determined to go through this alone."

"I didn't realise you smoked, that's all."

"Sod off. I don't. You drive me to it, you arsehole."

They sat there in silence for a few minutes, smoking. Anoush pulled her long cardigan around herself tightly. There was hardly a breeze, but it was seasonally chill and with her thin frame, she was susceptible to the cold. Jeff felt a sliver of guilt for making her sit outside with him, but since the ban, patients were obliged to sit outside to smoke, which most of them did.

"I don't know, it's… It seems so real when I'm there, but it's not, is it. It's just a psychosis. I don't see what point there'd be describing it, it's not real."

"Maybe something in it would be a clue as to what's triggering it, I don't know."

Jeff thought about the pale woman, but for some reason he didn't want to say anything about her out loud. For someone temporarily residing in a mental hospital, Jeff felt surprisingly reluctant to appear insane. Instead, he just said, "I don't think it works like that. It's a psychosis, there's no pattern to it, no message. I'm just seeing mad shit I can't explain that isn't real, and then I stop seeing it and I'm back here."

"Back here. So, what you see is somewhere else."

Jeff sighed. Clearly Anoush wasn't going to let this go.

"China, I think. Some kind of war. In the future. Against…
against aliens." He snorted and scratched his head. "See?
I sound ridiculous."

Anoush put out her cigarette and reached over to him,
taking his hand.

"You don't sound ridiculous." Jeff opened his mouth
to protest, but Anoush pushed on. "You don't sound
ridiculous," she repeated. "You sound nuts, sure. But you
don't sound ridiculous."

Jeff laughed, then put his other hand on hers, bowed
his head and sobbed.

Once more, then, they pulled up outside Anoush's
flat. Once more, she helped him inside with his belongings.
Once more he stowed his bag next down to her couch
while she made tea. Looking around, he took in the
sparsely laden bookshelves, the crime novels and sci-fi
conspicuous by their absence.

"He's really gone this time then?"

"Who knows. I don't give a shit. He texted me last week,
asked if he could come and get a few bits. I told him to
take everything, that anything he left would be going to
the charity shop. I came home later to find most of his
stuff gone, so I kept my word, junked the rest and changed
the locks. He might come back, tail between his legs, but
he'll be shit out of luck if he does. Bastard can make his
own way in the world now, I'm done looking after him."

"One hopeless case at a time, eh?"

Anoush dropped onto the couch next to him and
nudged him in the ribs. "You said it, shitsack. Pizza?"

"You know, I'd kill for a decent burger."

"We could go Chinese…"

Jeff gave Anoush the dourest look he could muster.

"Is this seat taken?"

Jeff was sitting in a chain coffee shop. He'd come into

town to buy himself a notebook and was now racking his brain, trying to remember as much as possible about the visions, getting as much as he could down on paper. It was fractured, scraps, just odd words mostly, but the plan was if it happened again, when it happened again, if he kept the notebook with him, he might be able to get more down as he came out of it. He still didn't see what possible point there was to the exercise, but Anoush had suggested it to Doctor Singh, who had agreed with her. Jeff half-suspected that the doctor had agreed with Anoush purely so as to not disagree with her, but then what else was he doing right now?

Engaged as he was, he didn't look up, just waved his hand at the seat opposite as in indication of its availability. When nobody sat down, he looked up, to see a young woman grinning at him.

"Oh, hey."

"Jeff, right? I thought it… Bloody hell, you look rough." Sal's grin didn't exactly disappear, but it morphed into something a little strained.

Jeff rubbed at his beard ruefully. He was well aware that he looked terrible. Anoush had made a point of telling him how pale and drawn he looked, berating him for the spiky, ruffled state of his hair that he did nothing with. Which reminded him that he was also going to get a haircut in town, that might get her off his back for a while.

"Yeah, been an odd few weeks. You sitting?"

"Sure, yeah," Sal shook her head, pulling herself out of the slight daze that Jeff's zombified appearance had put her in. "So, what's going on?"

Jeff closed his notebook and put it in the inside pocket of his jacket. "Long story." He gestured dismissively. "Long, boring story."

Sal took a sip of the enormous coffee she'd bought before responding. "I've nowhere to be."

Jeff pursed his lips, looking at the young woman for a moment. She was, if anything, cuter than he remembered. Short, cropped hair, same hoodie, and was that a wrestling t-shirt she had on? Very little make-up, which he liked. Dark purple lipstick, not so much. Now that he thought about it, the blonde wasn't natural. She had a nice face, he decided. Her green eyes sparkled.

"Well, let's say you've met me at a very interesting time of my life…"

"*Fight Club* reference. There's a red flag if ever I saw one."

Jeff grinned.

Sal ended up coming with him to get his haircut. Turned out she really had nowhere to be, was just drifting around town after a friend had cancelled plans at the last minute. She was easy to talk to, easier than Anoush, he had to admit. She wasn't judgemental and didn't seem fazed by his confession that he was only recently discharged from a mental health facility. It transpired that she had a stepbrother who'd killed himself when she was a teenager, so the whole mental health thing was familiar territory. As he spoke about Jezz, and the future war in China, a few more details resurfaced, which he duly scribbled down in his notebook.

The conversation broadened, flowed and Jeff found a weight, one he hadn't even been fully conscious of, lifting from his shoulders. He laughed, properly, for the first time since he'd left the clinic. It seemed they had a fairly healthy crossover of mutual interests, books, films and the like. Sal made him feel good, easy; not carefree, exactly, but certainly less worn down. When he went into the barbers, she pointed at a Salvation Army shop opposite and went to peruse the second-hand books and records while she waited.

"Bloody hell, Jeff!"

He rubbed his hand over his freshly shaven scalp. "You like?"

"Well, it's certainly added to that fresh-out-of-the-gulag look you're cultivating."

"Nice."

"No, it's cool. Suits you."

He smiled ruefully. "Cheers. Figured it'd be easier to maintain."

"For sure. Can't believe you paid for that though. If I'd known that was what you were intending, I'd have taken you back to mine and done it myself."

"It wasn't planned. Just sat in the chair and when he asked me what I wanted, it just came out."

"Just came off, you mean. Well, it was an inspired decision, mate."

"What next, then?"

"I was thinking of catching a film. You in?"

"Why not?"

He texted Anoush to let her know he was going to be a while, but that he was okay, and then the pair headed off, Jeff smiling to himself as Sal casually slipped her arm in his.

"What the hell, Jeff?"

"You don't like it?"

Of course Anoush didn't like it, he'd been well prepared for her disdain.

"Well, I think it looks wonderful, darling. Very chic, very now." Anya, a glass of wine in one hand, pulled him close with the other and kissed him on the top of his head.

"He looks like a thug."

"Nonsense. He looks divine," Anya gushed, her arm still around her stepson as she turned to face her daughter. Anoush rolled her eyes and carried the crisps and dips she was holding through into the living room. "Don't listen to her, darling. She's just jealous." Anya kissed him again and then ushered him through the door, following behind.

The three of them sat on Anya's absurdly huge sofa. Anoush sat at one end, her back to the sidearm, facing the other two, and her feet tucked up beneath her. Jeff sat in the middle.

"So, who's this girl you went to the movies with?"

"Her name's Sal, I met her a while back, before my last episode. Ran into her again, hit it off. She had nothing to do this afternoon, neither did I, so we just hung out." Jeff shrugged. "That's it."

Anoush leaned forward and punched him on the arm. "You dog. Ha! Listen to how offhand he is, mama."

"Are you seeing her again, darling?"

Again, Jeff shrugged. "No plans to. She did take my number; said she'd text sometime. I dunno. It wasn't really, you know, charged or anything. We hit it off, but not like that. It was just nice to hang out. Nice to feel normal for a bit. To chat to someone."

"Oh, so her you can talk to," said Anoush, her tone sardonic. But she was smiling, and Jeff could see just the slightest hint of moistness in her eyes as she leaned forward and kissed his cheek, resting her arm over his shoulder as she did so. "I'm just glad you're talking, baby." She kissed him again and leaned back. "Are we watching this film then?"

Jeff reached for the remote on the coffee table and hit play.

The pub was moderately busy, for a Wednesday, but it didn't take much to find a table. Jeff folded his coat up, placing it on the bench next to where Sal was sitting. "What can I get you?"

"Gin, please."

Jeff gave her a thumbs up, cringing internally as he did so. It only took a few minutes to get served and Jeff was back at the table in no time, gin, beer and crisps bestowed upon the surface as if he were a subject proffering a gift to their monarch.

"Why thank you, good sir."

"Don't 'good sir' this fool." Jeff winced as Anoush appeared behind him, giving his shaven scalp a hearty rub. This hadn't been planned as a 'meet the family' date, it had just turned out that way. When he mentioned that his stepmother's klezmer band was playing at a nearby pub, Sal had pounced on the opportunity, pleading with him playfully until he acquiesced.

"Sal, this is my half-sister, Anoush. Anoush, Sal."

"Pleased to meet you… ooh," Sal was momentarily taken aback by the stick-thin blonde swooping down on the seat beside her, throwing her arms around her and kissing her on both cheeks.

"Delighted to meet you. Delighted to find out you're real, for a start. Jeff has a tendency to imagine company."

"Dammit, Anoush…"

She flapped a hand at him to shut him up. "It's okay, you told us she knows about you being a loony."

"Yeah, but I didn't warn her you were."

Anoush poked her tongue out at him, provoking a giggle from Sal. Comforting himself with the knowledge that in some senses it was as if the plaster had been ripped off swiftly, Jeff reached for his beer, only to nearly spill it as Anya descended on the table with, if anything, a more flamboyant entrance than her daughter.

"Darling, you came!"

"Of course he came, mother. He wanted to show off his *gelibter*."

"Have you been drinking?" Jeff was starting to smart under his half-sister's good humour.

"Children, children, behave." Anya, sensing Jeff's discomfort, gestured at them both to simmer down and placed her clarinet case on the table. "Sal, you must forgive my children, since their father died I can't do a thing with them. Stand up, let me see you."

Sal duly stood, unusually cowed by this force of nature and her immense hair. Anya wrapped her arms around her, kissed her and then stood back, holding Sal's shoulders as she looked her up and down.

"Jeffrey, she's a doll. Be kind to her."

"I'm going outside for a smoke, you coming?"

Sal, a wry grin on her face, wriggled out of Anya's grip and slipped out from behind the table. "It's lovely to meet you, Mrs Ginetti."

"And so well spoken, darling. You kids have fun, I'm going to go set up." She leant over the table and beeped Anoush on the nose. "Play nicely, darling."

Anoush grinned up at her. "I always play nice, mother dearest." Anya threw back her head and gave a single bark of laughter. Picking up her clarinet, she swept off to the far corner of the pub, showering her affection on those she passed that she knew.

Jeff offered Sal one of his cigarettes, but she declined, pulling her rolling paraphernalia from her jacket.

"Families, eh?" Sal was grinning.

Jeff smiled ruefully. "Can't live with them…"

"They seem lovely."

Jeff inhaled deeply and slowly exhaled a thick cloud of smoke.

"They are. They're nigh on unbearable at times, Anoush particularly, but I honestly don't think I'd be here without them." He scuffed his trainer against the pavement in thought. "I treated them both really badly when my dad was alive. Couldn't stand the fact he'd got married again, played up something chronic. And when he died, I practically walked away from them. Never wanted to see them again."

"What happened to change your mind?"

"Anoush did. Never gave up on building that bridge. Then when I started having problems, and she was the only one who stuck by me, I realised what I'd been so intent on throwing away. With Anya, too. Neither of them ever held it against me for a moment." Jeff wiped at his eyes and took another drag on his cigarette. "Dammit."

"It's okay," said Sal, reaching out and softly touching his arm. "I get that though, they seem… so loving."

"That they are." Jeff stretched his arms out, rolled his neck. "Honestly, I was barely old enough to really know my mother. Not as a person. But Anya's been more of a mum than a lot of people get from their actual mother. She's a saint. Utterly batshit crazy, but a saint."

Sal turned at the sound of an accordion-player warming up inside. "Did we ought to go in?"

"I'll be in in a minute. Just compose myself a bit." He twitched, an undertone in his voice that hadn't been there before. Sal didn't notice. Instead, she nodded, dropped her cigarette end in the bin, patted him on the arm and went in.

He watched her go, then turned back to look across the road to where a pale woman with short, almost white hair stood watching him. Jeff's whole body was tensed, the fight-or-flight instinct flooding his system with adrenaline.

The woman raised a hand to her mouth and, though Jeff couldn't hear her above the background noise of the city, the shake of her shoulders told him she was coughing. She put out her other hand to steady herself against a lamppost. Jeff binned his cigarette, spun on his heels and retreated into the pub.

"You okay?" Anoush frowned. The change in Jeff didn't escape her for a moment, and the way she asked the question made Sal look up too.

"I just saw her."

"Who?"

"The pale woman?" asked Sal.

Jeff nodded.

Anoush looked at Sal, cocked an eyebrow. Sal reached over and took Jeff's hand as he sat down but addressed Anoush. "It's a precursor. To an episode. There's a pale woman that Jeff sees just before he… goes."

The band chose that moment to launch into their first song, distracting the couple on the next table who had just started to stare at them. Sal pulled Jeff towards her and he compliantly shifted from the stool he'd flopped down on to the bench, where Sal guided him to sit between her and Anoush. Anoush put an arm around him as Sal took both his hands in both of hers.

"Breathe," instructed Sal. "No, not deeply. Deep breathing will increase the imbalance of oxygen in your bloodstream, that won't help. Breathe slowly and calmly. Through the nose."

"So he's about to have an episode?" asked Anoush, her voice a mixture of concern and confusion; confusion that this new arrival, this stranger, seemed to have a better idea of what was going on than she did.

"Possibly. I don't know. But let's see if we can stop him, hey?"

"I am here," said Jeff quietly.

Anoush started to stroke his head. "Sorry, babes."

"It's okay. I think we ought to leave."

"Where did you see her?" asked Sal.

"Outside. Across the road."

"And is she inside now?"

Jeff looked around, panicked at the idea. His head darted around for a moment, then he shook it. "No, I can't see her."

"Well, if she was outside, and she's not in here now, how about we stay here for a bit, yes?"

Jeff didn't sound sure as he replied, "Okay."

Anoush shared a glance with Sal, her appreciation of the level-headed new friend her brother had found evident in her eyes. Sal gave her a weak smile in return.

The band played on.

Jeff woke up, surprised to realise, after a moment, that he was lying in one of Anya's guest bedrooms. He lay there, staring at the ceiling. He'd seen the pale woman, yet he hadn't… gone? Had he? He felt the standard slight confusion of waking up in someone else's bed but, aside from that, he felt pretty sure it was only the morning after Anya's pub gig. And he had no sensation of being Jezz, or of having been in China. So, he hadn't had an episode?

There was a tentative knock at the door, and it opened slightly. Sal's face, hair dishevelled, peeped round the door. "Hey."

"Hey you". It was a face Jeff hadn't expected to see, but he found that he was very glad to.

"Can I come in?"

"Sure."

Sal slipped in through the narrow gap and closed the door quietly behind her. She was wearing one of Anoush's long t-shirts, red, and down to her knees, clearly having just got up. She tippy-toed over to the bed, lifted the duvet and slipped in next to him.

"You don't have to creep about; I think Anya's past the stage of worrying about me having girls in my room."

She lifted his arm and snuggled in under it. "I know, I just didn't want them to know you'd woken up yet. Thought it'd be nice to lay here for a bit."

Jeff nodded. "I'm seeing your vision."

"Speaking of which…?" The question didn't need to be clarified.

"Nope, nothing. I'm a bit confused by that, to be honest. Keep waiting for her to reappear, to go into one."

"Well, maybe this shows it doesn't have to go that way." Sal put a hand up on Jeff's chest and crooked a leg up to rest on his.

She felt nice under his arm, right. She seemed to fit perfectly, and Jeff felt a warm glow spread through his body. He hoped earnestly he wouldn't get an erection.

"Maybe. We'll see."

"Do you remember much of last night? You were very withdrawn."

"Yeah, I think so. We stayed for the gig, then came back here?"

"Pretty much. After we put you to bed, we stayed up talking a bit. I like your family. I was going to get an Uber home, but Anya insisted I stay."

"I'm glad she did." Jeff idly twirled a strand of Sal's hair around his finger.

"Me too."

They laid there for a little bit and Jeff became aware that Sal was drifting off to sleep again. He gently nudged her. "You nodding off?"

"Noooo," she gently protested, but her green eyes looked sleepy.

"Good, because I think we probably ought to get up. You know, before I get any ideas."

Sal punched him gently in the ribs. "Easy, tiger." She sat up and stretched. "Okay, I'm going to go find some breakfast."

"Probably best. I need the loo anyway."

"Didn't need to know that."

Sal slipped out from under the duvet again and made the same, cute pantomime of tip-toeing back to the door. Looking back over her shoulder, she gave him a wink, flashed her knickers and left.

Jeff grinned, took a deep breath and rubbed his eyes. He went to get up, then realised he had better wait a couple of minutes.

He debated going downstairs for a cup of tea and maybe a cigarette, but he was vaguely aware of a slight whiff of body, so decided he'd sneak a quick shower first. The bathroom was just opposite so he shuffled in, yawning, and crossed the room to look in the mirror.

Jeff stared at the dismal sight facing him. The shaved scalp merely added to the impression that he'd recently been released from an asylum in the 1900s. His beard, now significantly longer than the stubble on his head, was patchy and grey. He'd lost weight, he realised, and his eyes looked alarmingly bloodshot. It felt as if he'd had a good night's sleep, but he clearly needed more than a few of those, and he realised that Anoush's couch was probably not the best place to get it. He didn't want to go home. Frankly, he felt like getting rid of the flat altogether. Maybe it was time to bite the bullet and see if Anya would let him stay for a while. He gave himself a rueful half smile. As if that was a question he didn't know the answer to. He took a deep breath and exhaled slowly, staring at himself as if there were some sort of clue to what was going on etched into the lines of his face.

Naturally, he drew a blank. He went over to the shower, reached in and set it running. The room started to steam up almost immediately. *Damn, Anya's shower is amazing*, he thought to himself as he always did, *I ought to move in for that alone*. He pulled off his t-shirt and stepped out of his shorts. Checking the temperature of the shower, he hopped in and flinched mildly at the hot water.

It was fine though, once you got used to it. He stood there for a minute, just enjoying the warmth, then reached for the shampoo. Unused to his look, he put far too much on and the lather ran down into his eyes. Cursing under his breath, he held his face up to the stream.

The door opened.

"Hey! I'm in here!" Jeff called out, not looking round. He instinctively turned slightly to the wall so his sister, or stepmother, wouldn't see his junk. Needlessly, as the shower cubicle was completely steamed up now, he realised.

The door closed again.

Jeff squeezed a blob of shower gel onto his hand and started to rub it over his chest. The gel was one of those super masculine for-men brands that seemed to think men wouldn't wash with anything that smelled of flowers. Anya must have it on standby for him visiting. It gave off a weird smell, almost like engine oil.

He became aware of light footsteps crossing the bathroom.

"Sal?"

He experienced a stirring. This, he had not expected.

"Sal? Whatcha doin'?"

He could just make out the shape of her through the shower screen, the red of Anoush's t-shirt, topped off by an indistinct blonde shape.

"It may have escaped your notice, but I'm having a shower here. I'm not exactly dressed for company."

The red shape rose up and Jeff realised Sal was taking the shirt off. He swallowed nervously. He was fully alert now, standing to. Sal wriggled out of the shirt and threw it to one side.

"You should know, I'm starting to get ideas here..."

Sal stepped forward again and her hand reached out to pull the shower screen open. Jeff, nervously grinning to himself, stood facing her. The door to the shower opened.

It wasn't Sal...

7

Jeff sat bolt upright. What the fuck? He twisted his head round, trying to work out where he was. His back was killing him, and he was slouched on the floor, tucked up awkwardly, around a… toilet? He was in a toilet cubicle, clutching the bowl, the tightness of the space giving him the sensation of waking in a coffin.

"Sal!"

There was noise coming from beyond the room he was in, but Jeff couldn't identify it. Voices, music of some sort, barely audible under an overwhelming staccato clatter. Where the hell was he?

"Anoush!"

The floor he was on was wet and he registered an unpleasant smell of stale piss. The toilet he was wrapped around wasn't, he realised, in Anya's bathroom. This wasn't Anya's house at all. He was in a toilet cubicle, and a particularly grimy, unpleasant one at that.

He grimaced as he used the toilet bowl as leverage to haul himself to his feet. He collapsed onto the seat and sat there for a moment, panting. Coughing, he spat up a thick glob of phlegm that landed on the cubicle wall and slowly, like treacle, slid downwards.

It was gunfire. The noise outside that was drowning everything else out was gunfire. Jeff looked down at his clothes, the green fatigues and heavy boots.

Oh.

Jezz looked up. Was he still in the Ziyang bar he'd crashed out in? How long had he been here? Hadn't the owner come looking for him when he hadn't reappeared? Fuck sake, what was going on here?

He lurched, unsteady on his feet, out of the toilet cubicle, practically falling against the door of the bathroom. His sudden appearance terrified the bar owner, who was curled up in the corner of the room under a sink. The owner whispered frantically at Jezz in Cantonese but although he had a rudimentary grasp of some of the language, Jezz was far too disorientated to understand a word of what the man was saying.

"English? English?"

The bar owner just looked at him, terror in his eyes, pointing at the door.

"Eltiy'ch!"

Oh shit.

Jezz slowly, carefully opened the door of the bathroom, just a crack, and peeked out. The bar owner, Li Wei, apparently, stood behind him, gripping his shoulders. Jezz tried to ignore the irritation he was feeling at the man's proximity. The last thing he needed was a terrified civilian latching onto him but, at the same time, Jezz wasn't a monster. This was a fellow human scared out of his wits. Jezz hoped he'd maybe be able to get the man to safety and then find his way back to his unit.

The bar was empty. Okay, not empty, but there was no one alive in there. Half a dozen bodies littered the floor, lying amongst the broken furniture and shattered glass. Virtually all the glass had been shot out of the front windows. The door was hanging on its hinges. Most of the bottles behind the bar were smashed. Jezz stuck his head a tiny bit further around the door. Then he froze.

Two Eltiy'ch, their lower set of arms holding their alien weapons while their upper set gestured around them wildly, stood in the street outside the bar. Their mandibles were clattering furiously, the short antennae on their heads animated. Jezz had never seen one this close before, not in daylight. It took a moment to process the sight, so utterly alien did the Eltiy'ch appear.

If he had to guess, Jezz would imagine they were arguing over where they were, the direction they should be going in. He had a momentary flashback to arguing with Price about the same thing, back in the plaza where this all started. Half-close your eyes, it could be the same argument. But he was aware of the futility of interpreting their body language through human filters. This could be a mating ritual for all he knew. He could only hope they'd finish whatever it was quickly and fuck off.

He pulled his head back until he could barely see them, then waited, watching them. Behind him, Li Wei starting chattering at him again, prompting Jezz to spin around. He clasped his hand over the Chinese man's mouth.

"Don't. Say. A. Word." He glared at the bar owner, letting his face communicate the message that his words would probably fail to. Li Wei froze. Jezz turned back to the door.

Damn. He couldn't see the Eltiy'ch. He'd wanted them to go, but he'd also wanted to *watch* them go. Jezz leaned further out of the bathroom door, slowly. He breathed a small sigh of relief when he saw the two Eltiy'ch, now joined by a third, tramp off down the street.

Jezz turned back to Li Wei. Putting his finger to his lips, he held his other hand up to indicate that the bar owner was to stay put. Then he eased himself through the bathroom door. Keeping low, he made his way into the bar.

He picked his way gingerly though the broken glass littering the floor. Stepping carefully over the corpses, he ducked down behind the bar and counted to ten. Then, he slowly peeked over the top of the counter. There was no one to be seen on the street from where he was, human or Eltiy'ch. Jezz crouched down again.

So, the Eltiy'ch had advanced into the city. The emptiness on the street suggested either that he was now far behind enemy lines or, hardly a brighter prospect, that he was smack in the middle of a confused front line. Jezz figured it must be the latter, given the three Eltiy'ch outside, and the fact that the bar owner had still been hiding in the bathroom. Jezz was shivering slightly in his coat, but that could be adrenalin. He was cold, but this was not the biting, inhuman cold the Eltiy'ch were able to manipulate into the environment wherever they conquered. Besides, he reasoned, he couldn't have been passed out in the bathroom for that long without being found. Surely the bar owner would have found him before now if he'd been there for any length of time. Jezz wondered at the disconnect between time passed and time imagined in that other place. He wished he had a pen and paper on him to try to get down what he could remember, before it disappeared into the fog of his memory. Something he should have thought of after his previous episodes. Right now, his current predicament was a little more pressing.

He quickly scanned the shelves behind, then under the bar. Bingo! He picked up a revolver the owner kept under the register. After checking to see if it was loaded, Jezz tucked it in his waistband. One box of bullets, half-empty, sat next to it, so he pocketed them, but there was no sign of any more. It wouldn't get them far, but it might get them far enough.

Jezz once again checked the street. Seeing no sign of life, he hesitantly came out from behind the bar to give the bodies a once over. Two of the corpses belonged to Korean soldiers and Jezz had to stifle a whoop as he found their rifles. Now this was more like it. Magazines, too. Perfect.

He went back into the bathroom. Li Wei was staring at him, desperation in his eyes.

"You spoke English when I came in. You speak English?"

Li Wei nodded but didn't respond verbally.

"Okay. Stop me if I go too fast, or you don't understand what I'm saying. Yes?"

The bar owner nodded.

"There are no Eltiy'ch out on the street. We're safe at the moment, but we can't stay here. I have to get back to my unit. Understand?"

Another nod.

"I will take you with me, to safety. Okay?"

The bar owner nodded again, more vigorously. "Thank you, thank you…"

Jezz held up his hand. "It will be dangerous. You," he pointed at the bar owner, "must do everything I," pointing at himself, "say. Yes?"

"Yes, I do what you say, yes, yes."

Jezz put his finger to his lips again. "Number one. You don't talk unless you absolutely have to. We have to be very, very quiet." An image of Elmer Fudd came into his mind, unbidden.

Li Wei put a hand over his own mouth and nodded. Jezz allowed himself a fleeting smile.

"Good. Number two, can you use this?" He held up one of the Korean rifles.

Li Wei's eyes widened. He shook his head, backing away from Jezz.

"Don't worry, it's fine." Jezz held out his hands to placate the other man. He slung one of the rifles over his shoulder and put the other one at his feet. Then he reached for the handgun he'd found behind the bar. He held it out to the bar owner. "Is this yours?"

Li Wei nodded. The bar owner tentatively took the weapon from Jezz.

"I hope we won't have to use them. Okay? And you are not to shoot at *anything* unless I shoot first. This is very important. I need you to understand that."

"I don't shoot til you shoot first."

Jezz nodded. The Chinese man was clearly terrified. Nevertheless, he seemed to have a good head on his shoulders and was happy to take Jezz's lead. Jezz counted his blessings. He could have so easily been trying to talk down a hysterical mess. Li Wei's composure, such as it was, was admirable.

More importantly, it increased both their chances of getting out of this alive.

The buildings around the bar were largely intact. There was a lot of shot-out glass on the street, but the structures were sound, mostly. Largely an infantry push, then, without the softening up barrage of artillery that would have flagged the imminent action. Probably caught everyone by surprise, allowing the Eltiy'ch to overrun the human line like quicksilver. Or maybe, and Jezz was grasping at straws here, just a tiny incursion by a few raiding Eltiy'ch units, and they'd stumble across human forces any minute, please God.

He and Li Wei moved cautiously from doorway to doorway. The bar owner was too scared for them to run proper covering manoeuvres, so Jezz settled for letting the civilian stay one hiding spot behind him, waving him forward when he deemed it safe. In this manner, they made it half a dozen blocks without seeing anyone. Anyone alive, that is.

The scale of human loss was less than Jezz had feared, but it was still hard not to be sickened by the sight of corpses littering the street. Already, packs of stray dogs were out looking for carrion. It was all Jezz could do to stop himself from trying to protect the dignity of the recently deceased, but to antagonise a pack would only serve to bring them to the attention of anyone nearby. Or anything.

Jezz had briefly considered checking for survivors in the shops and apartments they passed. However, he had no idea if there might be Eltiy'ch in the buildings. Besides, guiding one civilian to safety was already costing him enough time and compromising his ability to react. Even two or three more would be impossible to manage, even if they were as together and pliant as Li Wei. Which, let's face it, was unlikely. It was one thing feeling unable to leave the bar owner to his fate once they'd been thrown together, but he wasn't equipped or prepared for any large-scale rescue effort on his own. Anyone else out there would just have to take their own chances.

Doorway by doorway, block by block, hour by hour, they inched their way across the city. The nature of urban warfare meant that the front line could be anywhere. Jezz was painfully aware that, just a couple of blocks in either direction and they might have met up with human forces hours previously. But there was no way to second guess that. All he could do was head away from the direction the Eltiy'ch had come from and hope that they'd make it.

It was dark by the time they finally reached safety. By that time, they'd spent eight hours making their way across the city, one shelter at a time. They'd had to stop more than Jezz would have liked, to accommodate Li Wei. The frightened civilian seemingly had a limit for how much scuttling from doorway to doorway he could manage at a time before he started muttering to himself and waving his gun about, startled by the slightest noise.

When he started to waver, Jezz would pull them into an abandoned shop or bar and give him a chance to regain his composure. They'd wait ten, sometimes fifteen minutes. The bar owner would say "Sorry, sorry," Jezz would give him a reassuring pat on the shoulder, and with a pained smile he would then hold his finger to his lips again, the signal to move out.

Overall Jezz was full of admiration for the bar owner. On the single occasion they'd almost ran into a Eltiy'ch patrol, Li Wei had frozen, fully pressed against the wall of the doorway he was stood in. He waited there patiently, silently, until the alien soldiers moved on. Even then he didn't move or make a sound as Jezz moved farther on, waiting until the soldier came back, satisfied the way was clear.

Eventually they came across a street that had been fully barricaded. Jezz, his own nerves nearly shredded by now, barely stopped himself from weeping when he saw movement behind it and realised that they'd reached the human forces.

Even more fortuitously, it was his own forces. Any humans, obviously, would have been fine, Jezz was in no place to be choosy. But, not knowing the situation, Jezz had been slightly worried that they'd find themselves with some Korean or Malay, or even Indian, division, cut off from his own people. He would have had to just fall in with the foreign troops, spend the rest of the war with them, even. But it was all good. His own unit was close by, he was told. He could reunite with Teemu and Price in the morning.

The bar owner was escorted to a safe civilian zone, after a tearful, on his part, goodbye with Jezz. Li Wei grabbed Jezz's hand in both of his and shook and shook, not wanting to let go. "You save me, you save me. You come back, you drink for free, for life. You save me."

Jezz smiled, wearily, at the other man. Putting his free arm on the man's shoulder, he gave it a strong squeeze.

"You did well, Li Wei. You did really well. Take care, my friend."

The corporal stood with them gave Jezz an apologetic look as he gently prized the bar owner off him, pulling him away and helping him up into the back of a truck. Jezz stood waving as the truck drove off, Li Wei crying and waving in the back.

"What now?"

The corporal turned back to him. "You want to get back to your unit now, or get some sleep first?"

"I think sleep."

Jezz started back at the face in the mirror, the faint memory of Jeff having done the same in the back of his mind. He'd had a good ten hours' sleep, straight through, in a hotel room a few blocks from the barricade. He hadn't even pissed the bed. Outside, he could hear the movement of soldiers, and the shouted orders of officers. They were gearing up for a counterattack.

The same corporal from yesterday had apologetically woken him up half an hour before. "We let you rest as long as we could, but the company's getting ready to move out. Captain Morello didn't think it'd be a good idea to let you wake up and find us all gone. Thought it might freak you out. Besides, he thinks you probably need to report back to your own unit soon."

Jezz reassured her that he understood as he got up. The corporal gave him a rundown of recent events as Jezz made himself coffee.

It turned out that Jezz had correctly assessed the situation the day before. The lack of a pre-incursion artillery bombardment had meant the attack had caught them completely by surprise. Both military and civilian casualties had been high. But the incoming forces hadn't been numerous, and Command was positive about the chances of their countermeasures being successful. They were still wary of being lured into a trap, however, so the plan was only to push back as far as the Tuo River. The river would make a natural defensive line.

After the corporal had left, Jezz took a shower. Then he stood examining himself again in the mirror. Unshaven, unkempt, but hair at least clean now. Eyes still tired, skin still pale. Skinnier than was normal for him. He didn't much care for his reflection, but boy was he glad to see it. The previous day had taken an enormous toll on his nerves. The fact he had woken up today in a clean bed, with a shower and coffee, was more than he'd dared hope during his and Li Wei's desperate flight through the city.

Jezz got dressed and sat on the bed, finishing off his coffee and smoking a cigarette from the pack the corporal had kindly left him. She had been cute, Jezz was still himself enough to notice, but his thoughts, as soon as they strayed into that area, went straight to Nora. Damn, she was probably nearly home by now, he remembered. No, not damn. He hoped she was, that she had got out safely and was now putting this whole shitshow behind her. But the thought that he'd missed his chance to say goodbye stung. Not so much because they had fucked. He had some difficulty getting his head around that, but realistically, he had to admit that it had less to do with the surfacing of previously hidden passions and more to do with two people reaching for some final approximation of intimacy before they most probably died. No, the sting came from the fact they had fought alongside each other for months. She was, first and foremost, his comrade. One of his crew.

Dropping his cigarette in the dregs of his coffee, Jezz stood up. His crew. He should probably find them.

It was a crisp, fresh morning in Ziyang. A definite chill in the air, for sure, but a natural one, not the enforced, unnatural cold of encroaching Eltiy'ch territory. Jezz hitched a ride on a jeep heading back to Command HQ, jumping off when the driver told him they were passing close to where his company were making ready.

He trotted down a side street in the direction he was pointed which opened out into a large square. A collection of tanks was arranged in the open area, many of their engines already turning over.

Spotting Major Bartley, Jezz reported in, giving a clipped, brief account of his whereabouts the past twenty-four hours. Bartley seemed entirely uninterested as he told him where to find his tank amongst the group in the square.

Towards the back of the group, it seemed. Engine still quiet, Price was on the hull, shouting down into the interior.

"Trouble, captain?"

Price looked down at him as if looking at a ghost. It was a moment before he could speak.

"You missed Nora."

"I know." Jezz told him he'd been out for a walk, got caught in the Eltiy'ch incursion. As with Bartley, he didn't tell Price there'd been another episode. He merely asserted the facts, that he'd been caught out by the Eltiy'ch advance and had to make his own way back, escorting a civilian survivor.

When he'd finished, Price gave him a curt nod. "I'm glad you're okay."

Teemu's head poked up out of the turret, "This boy's an imbecile, and we've seriously got to take another one on to replace Jezz?"

"Doesn't look like it now," replied Price, jerking a thumb over his shoulder.

Teemu looked down and, seeing Jezz, muttered "About fucking time," before disappearing back into the tank.

"Engine?"

"Hydraulic leak," answered Price. "Shouldn't take long. We roll out in half an hour. You eaten?"

Jezz shook his head.

"There's a canteen set up in that bodega over there," Price waved a spanner towards a corner of the square. "Get us some rolls and coffee."

Jezz saluted and jogged off.

The column rolled out an hour or so later. Price's estimation had been ambitious, given the state of their hydraulic leak and, even then, they weren't the last to fire up their engine. The company they now found themselves in was a ragtag collection of armour from various outfits, brought together as their numbers dwindled. There were, however, finally some rumours of reinforcements. Regular army and private militias were said to be crossing the border from India. For now, though, the defence of Ziyang lay in the hands of the survivors of the combat in the east, and there wasn't a single outfit left in existence that hadn't had to be absorbed into another.

Their tank was a microcosm of this. Teemu was in the driver's seat, Price where he usually rode before contact was made, with his head out the top of the main turret. He was, Jezz and Teemu were convinced, going to end this war with a bullet in the head. It was surely inevitable that at some point, that first point of contact would be a Eltiy'ch sniper picking off the exposed officer. Neither of them had tried arguing the point with Price, however. They knew the man well enough to understand how pointless that would be.

Nora's place, however, was filled by a Swiss kid they'd been assigned, a survivor of another tank where the rest of the crew had perished. He barely spoke English, in fact barely spoke at all. But when Price pointed him at the main gun and indicated that he should load it, the kid sprung to and had it ready for firing in no time. Even Price had been impressed.

Jezz was in the front compartment. Like Price, he rode standing up, waist high in the front hatch. He'd found an old Korean helmet that almost fit him, so was wearing that and holding one of the Korean rifles he'd brought back from the bar. He wasn't usually so laissez-faire going into action, but he was feeling pretty invincible after the events of the past twenty-four hours. Besides which, the inside of the tank had started to reek. Tempting as it was to point at the new kid, Jezz knew it was Teemu, the great bear of a man relishing the absence of Nora and her constant moaning about hygiene. Nora 2, as their new loader was soon christened, seemed oblivious to the smell.

The column drove about half a mile before it split up, taking a variety of designated side streets and main thoroughfares, in an effort to flush the bugs out from whatever ratholes they may be hiding in. Jezz stayed up top, sweeping his rifle back and forth, scanning the surrounding buildings for any movement. Periodically, he or Price would call out, pointlessly asking if the other had seen anything.

They were just a few streets away from the river when Price ducked back inside the tank. Moments later, the engine slowed up. They came to a complete stop on a crossroads. Jezz, still panning left and right with his Korean rifle, shouted back, "What's the score, Price, what's going on?"

Price hoisted himself fully out of the hatch. Slithering down the hull, he came to a stop beside Jezz. He spoke quietly, "Command thinks if there's no Eltiy'ch this side of the river, they'll be waiting on the other side to pound on us the moment we appear on the quays. We're waiting here until we get the signal to roll out full speed along the last stretch, and come out firing."

"We far enough back that they won't have heard us coming already?"

Price shrugged. "Fuck knows. The bugs might have super-hearing. They could be listening to us right now from Beijing for all we know. But we're far enough away that they may not have heard us, and close enough that when we do go full throttle, we'll be out in the open before they can react."

Jezz put his rifle down on the hull and took out a packet of cigarettes. He offered one up to Price, partly as a tacit way of asking approval to light up without having to say the word 'permission'. They were supposed to conduct themselves like regular army, but there was a wide distrust of needless protocol in the militia they'd taken their shares out in.

Surprisingly, Price accepted the cigarette, shifting from a crouching position to sitting, legs stretched out, on the hull. He lit up then leaned back on one elbow, transferring the cigarette to his leaning arm so he could stroke his moustache with the other.

"You really think they're all the other side of the river?" Jezz asked.

"Hell if I know. I've given up trying to figure out what the bugs are up to. It'd be hard enough with a human enemy, but these are aliens. Command don't even know *if* they think, let alone how. I keep waking up every morning with the thought that they might have just all up and left Earth again over night. Then again, they could rain down a million nukes on us at any moment. There's no understanding them, Jezz. No, we just got to keep killing them until they stop killing us."

Jezz nodded, slowly. "I guess so." He let his gaze slowly track over the surrounding buildings. He could now see tanks in either direction, parked up as they were, at parallel junctions. Behind them, there was the sound of feet lightly running up to them. Infantry. Price leaned out to be sure, although it sounded obviously too fast to be Eltiy'ch.

A sergeant, regular A., trotted up to them and saluted. "Sergeant Edwards, sir. We're your infantry. 86 company."

Price gave an approximation of a salute, cigarette still in his mouth. "Thank you, sergeant."

The sergeant stood there for a moment, as if expecting some kind of orders. Then, realising he wasn't getting any, he trotted back to his men.

"Like I know what the fuck to do with an infantry unit," Price muttered.

They waited there for about fifteen minutes. After Price had finished his cigarette, he pulled himself up and retook his position. Jezz, suddenly needing to take a piss, signalled to Price that he was hopping out. Price gave him the okay but told him not to go too far. They could be moving out at any moment.

Jezz crossed the street in the direction of the river. He figured if they did need to roll, then if he was in front of the tank he could jump on before they picked up speed, rather than make them wait for him to run back.

He stood the other side, so modest, of a mailbox and started to relieve himself. It had been a sunny day when he'd caught up with the unit, but it was looking hazy now, as if a mist was rolling in from the river. He looked up and down the street as he urinated. Then, as he dried up, he shook himself and zipped up his pants.

He took out another cigarette and lit it, standing in the street for a minute to check out the vacant shops around him. Mostly small businesses. They weren't currently sitting in a flourishing district. Not that there were any of those now, Jezz thought to himself. But these were all small bars, small markets, vape shops, noodle shops, bootleg clothing shops and the like. He tried on a pair of sunglasses from a spinning rack outside the store he'd pissed by.

Behind him, Price was yelling something, no doubt to hurry the fuck up and get back in the fucking tank. There was no engine noise though, from theirs or any of the nearby tanks. They weren't moving out, Price was just getting jittery. Jezz gave him a wave, then tried on another pair of sunglasses.

Something moved in the street behind him. He spun round, the price tag on the nose of the sunglasses banging irritatingly on his face. He brought his rifle up and was on the verge of opening fire before he realised it wasn't the enemy.

A local man was staggering down the street, holding his throat and coughing. Jezz looked back in the direction the man had come from, towards the river. Something wasn't right, the mist was very dark… Shit, Jezz tore the glasses off and looked again. The mist wasn't dark, but it was thick, and rolling down the street towards where they were waiting to advance. A rough, oily smell was wafting towards him on the breeze. The man, still coughing, fell to his knees, calling out hoarsely to Jezz in Mandarin.

But Jezz wasn't listening to him. Not now that he could make out what Price was shouting.

"GAS! JEZZ! GAS!"

Shitshitshitshit… Jezz spun around and started running, feet pounding on the tarmac, back to the tank. He didn't look back to see how fast the huge gas cloud was moving, or to see what had happened to the Chinese man.

He reached the tank and Price, already kitted out in his facemask, threw Jezz's down to him. Jezz dropped his rifle and struggled with his mask, pulling at the fastenings which weren't, fucking, undoing… there! He pulled it on and refastened it, checking the fit before reaching down again for his rifle and jumping up onto the hull.

The engine was rumbling now. Price, not waiting for the call to proceed, had decided that the gas cloud meant one thing and one thing only. A full Eltiy'ch advance. They planned to lay waste to Ziyang, today. Well fuck them, thought Price. He was shouting into his radio as Jezz dropped into his targeting chair, pulling the hatch down close above him.

"SWISS! WE READY TO GO?"

Nora 2 shouted something back at him, which Jezz took to be an affirmative, and he flicked on the targeting imager. The crossroads flickered into life on the screen in front of him. The image was small, but crystal clear, HD. It was the one bit of kit where Price had insisted they not skimped on the cost. Jezz gave the gun, and therefore the camera fixed to it, an experimental turn from left to right. "Online, chief!

But moments later, he shouted, "Shit, the cloud, I can't see shit out there!"

Price wasn't going to sit around waiting to be swarmed over. "I'm rolling!"

"Acknowledged," Jezz responded. Technically, even as Commander, the decision to go into battle had to be a unanimous one, for the militia corps. Especially if your tank was taking the decision to do so unilaterally. But Price was right, Jezz knew. They could sit here and be overrun by the Eltiy'ch in a matter of minutes, or they could roll on and maybe crash through the front line of the fuckers before they knew what hit them.

The tank lurched, as Teemu let out a Viking bellow of appreciation for action. Even Nora 2 joined in with a cheer of something or other in French.

This is it, Jezz thought to himself. This is fucking it.

They rolled forward, Teemu relying on GPS, driving blind in the gas cloud. Jezz fired a couple of short-range shells into the cloud, then switched to the forward machine gun, letting off controlled bursts. He had no idea if he was hitting anything, but if the gas attack *was* a cover for a Eltiy'ch advance, their front line would suffer for it.

Gas started infiltrating the tank almost immediately, making Jezz shiver in recollection of the outcome of the last Eltiy'ch gas he'd been exposed to. Judging by the man who'd stumbled out of the cloud, this wasn't a phero-chem attack, just a nasty physical one. Still, Jezz silently thanked the regular A. for their top-of-the-line facemasks.

Then it came, the angry pang of gunfire on the hull. The weight and momentum of the tank meant there was no indication of whether or not they'd rolled over any of the aliens, but fingers crossed. They were about half a klick from the river, so Teemu rolled on. The gunfire started to dissipate as they broke through the Eltiy'ch line.

"That doesn't feel like many of them," shouted Price over the engine.

"We're coming through the cloud," Jezz called back. On his screen, the view from the front camera was starting to take shape again. They were still rolling down the centre of the carriageway. Here and there Jezz caught fleeting glimpses of alien figures running to get out of their way. Jezz swept the street in front of them with the machine gun, grimacing with satisfaction as a number of aliens dropped.

"Shit!" yelled Teemu. The tank abruptly lurched forward at an angle. Something hit Jezz in the back of the head as everything in the cabin that wasn't tied down flew forward.

"What the hell?"

"Tank trap! The fuckers have blown pits in the road! Everybody out! Full alert, we've got bugs out there!"

Jezz swore as he unstrapped himself from his seat. Grabbing his rifle, he pushed up at the main hatch. He steeled himself, then scrambled up and out onto the hull.

He didn't stop to take anything in as he emerged, jumping down off the hull and dropping into the wide trench the tank had rolled into. Thankfully, it wasn't too deep. Just deep enough to stop their tanks. No doubt in part the purpose of the gas attack was also to mask the traps. Gunfire rang out in the street; the Eltiy'ch clearly positioned to finish off anyone they caught in their trap. Jezz crawled to the front of the trench, using it as cover as he carefully raised his head just enough to look out.

The gas cloud was still dispersing. Visibility was less limited, the street around him coming in and out of focus as the remnants of the chemical attack lingered in ribbons in the breeze. Seeing a pair of Eltiy'ch positioned in a shop doorway, Jezz brought his rifle up and fired a quick burst, felling one of them. He ducked back down as the other returned fire.

Nora 2 appeared beside him, the skinny kid in his facemask now virtually indistinguishable from his waiflike predecessor.

"Where are the others?"

The boy waved his hand towards the tank, then stuck his head above the lip of the trench. Jezz yanked him back down, just in time to save him from being mowed down by the Eltiy'ch in the nearby doorway.

"Fuck sake! Bugs out there!"

"'ow many?" It was the first time Jezz had heard the boy speak. His accent was thick, his voice surprisingly deep.

"No idea. There's one in cover just over there," Jezz held up one finger, then pointed, "but there's almost certainly others."

As if to confirm his statement, gunfire erupted on the far side of the road. Price and Teemu, presumably, and the Eltiy'ch in response.

Instinctively hoping that the gunfire would prove a momentary distraction, Jezz stuck his rifle back over the top of the trench and fired in the direction of the one Eltiy'ch he knew the whereabouts of. It paid off, the alien crumpling to the floor in the doorway.

"Run!"

Jezz took off down the trench towards the side of the road. Scrambling up over the side, he threw himself into a doorway. More gunfire erupted, but he made it safely. As he did so, Nora 2 slammed into him from behind, sending both of them crashing through the door into the small shop beyond. Jezz rolled back to the door, taking up a firing stance.

Outside he could see more and more of the street as the breeze dispersed the gas cloud further. The tank was a forlorn sight, pitched into the trench, useless to them. Probably recoverable, but not during a firefight. They'd have to wait until this was done and, with any luck, they'd pushed the Eltiy'ch back over the river.

He couldn't see Teemu or Price, but the occasional chatter of gunfire proved that at least one of them was still alive and engaging the Eltiy'ch. Jezz thought about shouting out to them, but realised it would achieve nothing, except to give his position away.

The gunfire stopped. An eerie silence filled the street.

"Dammit, now what?"

"Quoi?"

Jezz had almost forgotten about Nora 2. Turning to face him, he noticed for the first time that there was blood trickling from a wound on the boy's forehead. Jezz pointed at it. The boy wiped at his face. Not a bullet wound, Jezz realised. More likely he'd hit his head as the tank pitched. He pointed at the doorway, and at Nora 2's gun. The boy nodded and took up Jezz's position at the door. Jezz begun a quick search of the shop, to see if there was anything of use.

The shop was a local minimart, thank goodness. It would have been just his luck to roll into a bootleg fashion store. There was a small supply of basic first aid stuff behind the counter, which he raided for a bandage that he tossed at Nora 2. Then he swore at the fact his pack was still in the tank. This would have been a perfect chance to stock up on cigarettes. Technically looting, but the chances of the owner coming back were slim to none. Jezz tore open a packet and lit one, stuffing the rest of the pack and a few others into the pouches on his fatigues. He moved on to the snack food.

Suddenly, the door to the back of the shop flew open, and Jezz nearly lost control of his bladder. Standing there, mandibles clacking furiously, was the ugly black form of an Eltiy'ch soldier. It wasn't armed, but it lurched towards him so fast that Jezz didn't have a chance to bring his own rifle to bear. Behind him, Nora 2 screamed as the creature tackled Jezz to the floor, smothering him.

Jezz gagged as the rank oily stench of the alien filled his airways. His facemask would filter any toxins out, but the smell was still getting through, burning his nose and throat. He tried throwing the alien off, but the damned thing was so heavy. Punching didn't work either. Its chitinous outer shell was like punching a brick. Jezz remembered the combat knife he carried strapped to his ankle, but the fucking thing was out of reach…

"Help me!" he yelled, but his cry was drowned out by gunfire coming from outside. Clearly Nora 2's shriek of terror had given them away. He probably had only seconds to get out from under this thing.

There was a thick, glutinous fluid dripping onto his forehead. Jezz realised the alien was injured. There was a hole in the thing's shell above what Jezz guessed were its …eyes? It far outweighed him, and he was struggling to breathe, but its upper limbs were clearly ineffectual for hand-to-hand combat. Either the angle was wrong, or the damned thing was just too weak, but what blows it was landing were negligible. Jezz was amazed the

Eltiy'ch didn't try to attack him with its mandibles, but hell, *he* wouldn't want to bite *it*, either.

He summoned up all his strength for one last roll and finally got a hand to his ankle. Pulling out his knife, he thrust upwards in one single motion. For a moment, the knife just skidded along the shell, and Jezz was convinced that that was that. If the bastard's shell was too hard to penetrate with a knife, the alien wouldn't have to land any kind of blow, it would just crush him to death. Then he felt something give, and a hot liquid gushed out over his hand.

If he thought the smell was bad before, it was nothing compared to this fresh wound. Jezz turned his head to the side, vomiting into his facemask. The creature stopped trying to strike him and rolled off. Jezz scrambled back on his haunches, pulling at his mask. He dragged it, painfully, over his ears and threw it to one side, gagging. If there was any of the gas left in the air, he may be a goner, but the only alternative was drowning in his own puke.

He threw up again, a thick viscous vomit that seemed to carry the acrid, oily taste of the creature. He was sitting at a slight angle, back against the counter. Holding his stomach with one hand, he wiped at his mouth with the other. He drew in huge gulps of air, not giving a shit if it was toxic. Across the floor, the Eltiy'ch lay, twitching; its chest plate rising and falling, legs kicking out feebly.

Jezz remembered seeing some tape on the shelves. He glanced over at Nora 2, but the boy was still facing out, rifle covering the street. The firing had stopped again and Jezz became aware of a background growl of heavier fire coming from the direction of the river. "Sounds like we pushed them back," he called out, wincing as the effort drew his attention to what felt like a handful of cracked ribs. Fuck, but that thing was heavy.

He grabbed a roll of heavy-duty tape from the shelf and turned back to the creature, approaching it gingerly. Its legs had stopped moving now; but its antennae were still moving to-and-fro. It half-heartedly lashed out a feeble arm, which Jezz easily avoided. He stared down at the alien thing, the invader. Funny. He'd been fighting and killing these things for months, but this was the first time he'd ever seen one up close.

It wasn't black, he realised, rather a sort of iridescent, dark green. It didn't have what you'd call feet; instead, the bottom half of the legs flared out into a pad that presumably was just wide enough to give stability. Jezz crouched down, and in one fluid motion grabbed both legs and wound the tape around them half a dozen times, biting the end off. He had no idea if it would hold or if the creature would just rip it off with one kick, but the thing just lay there, looking at him, the foul liquid still dribbling out of its forehead and from the fresh wound in its abdomen where Jezz had stabbed it.

One by one, he grabbed each of its arms and, gagging on the stench, taped it to the floor. He had no idea why he was doing this. He'd certainly never heard of anyone taking one of the things prisoner. But killing it on the battlefield, even in a fistfight, was one thing. Putting it down with a bullet while it lay there wounded? Jezz couldn't bring himself to.

When he was sure it was taped down securely, or at least as sure as he could be, Jezz fell back on his arse and stared at it. "Why the hell did you fuckers have to come here?" he whispered. Then he dragged himself over to the door to Nora 2.

The boy still lay there, aiming his rifle out of the door.

"Hey," said Jezz, coming up to the doorway.

Nora 2 didn't respond. Didn't even look up. Jezz pulled himself a bit further until he was leaning up against the doorframe.

Nora 2 was still wearing his mask but above it, between the top edge of the mask and the boy's hairline, a neat, round, bloody hole was just starting to dry up.

Jezz threw his head back, howling in anguish, and started to weep. He hadn't known this kid, not for more than a few hours, hadn't connected with him in any meaningful way. But as he sat there, breathing laboured from being crushed by a fucking *alien*, looking out at a city he'd never heard of in a country he'd never any intention of visiting, without a clue whether any of his friends were alive or dead, not having spoken to his parents in months, the death of this stranger, this fucking child, was a loss too far. "Where are you?" he yelled, for the first time wishing, praying, that the pale woman would appear and make this stop. He longed for that miserable other life where all he seemed to do was mope around being looked after by women. "Why don't you stop this?"

But the woman didn't appear, and Jezz could do nothing but lay there, weeping. So, he wept.

It was about thirty minutes later when Price stepped over the still-sobbing Jezz and entered the shop. He looked round at the shop, then caught sight of the Eltiy'ch, still taped to the floor.

"What the... fuck?"

Jezz, registering another presence for the first time, threw his arms out in half-hearted attempt to grab a weapon. Teemu crouched down and took his hands. "Easy, Jezz. It's us, you're okay."

Jezz looked up, his eyes staring at the big man blankly. Then recognition blossomed. "Teemu?" He turned his head. "Price? You guys... you made it."

"Jezz, what the fuck is that?"

Jezz leaned forward to look past Price's legs. He'd almost forgotten the alien was there.

"My prisoner." He slumped back against the door.

"You took it prisoner? What the fuck, Jezz? What do you expect me to do with that?"

"I dunno, I wasn't really thinking that far ahead," he mumbled. He was so tired. "Interrogate it?"

Price looked back at his comrade with genuine disbelief on his face. "*Interrogate* it? Do I look like Amy Adams?" Price shook his head, then turned back to the creature. He pulled out his pistol, took a step towards it and fired three rounds into its head.

Teemu stood. Reaching down, he helped Jezz to his feet, throwing Jezz's arm, the one not holding his ribs, over his shoulder. "Bloody hell, but you stink, boy. What is that?"

Jezz didn't answer.

Price picked up the tiny body of Nora 2 and followed them outside.

"Recovery team's on its way for the tank. We'll hitch a ride back to command."

Jezz sat on the gurney facing another tired doctor in another field hospital.

"So I hear your driver drove right into a Eltiy'ch tank trap," said the doctor in a breezy, conversational tone as he shone his penlight in Jezz's eyes. "Follow the light, please."

Jezz did as he was told but declined the invitation to chat. He was exhausted, but more than that he was numb. Since Price and Teemu had found him again he'd slumped into a melancholy state, unresponsive to any attempt by them to pull him out of himself. They'd taken him to the field hospital to get his physical injuries checked out and his ribs were now strapped up firmly. As a matter of protocol, the three of them were now being checked for signs of exposure to the Eltiy'ch chemical weapon.

"Open your mouth, please... That's great, okay."

The doctor switched off the penlight, rolled his chair back and made a few notes in the chart on the desk. He called for a nurse, who came in with a blood-kit.

"Okay, soldier, Nurse Willis is just going to take some blood, alright?"

Jezz nodded, his gaze on the floor. He barely seemed to notice as the nurse lifted his arm and swabbed it, didn't flinch as the needle went in. The doctor frowned. The nurse took three vials of blood, then quickly whipped a dressing over the spot as she withdrew the needle.

After she left, the doctor rolled his chair up to Jezz again.

"You experiencing any symptoms of phero-attack? Visual or audio hallucinations?"

Jezz shook his head.

"Any difficulty breathing, discomfort in the throat, headaches, dizziness?"

Again, Jezz silently shook his head.

The doctor looked at him for a moment.

"Humour me, soldier. I need you to say something, see that those vocal cords are still working. Are you here with me?"

Jezz looked up.

"I…" He shrugged forlornly. "I guess."

"You've had a hell of a day. I heard about the Eltiy'ch you fought. That must be a hell of a thing, being that close up to one. I don't blame you for being a little freaked out."

"We lost our loader." Jezz's eyes welled up, tears dropping onto his cheeks, trickling into his beard.

The doctor nodded. "I heard that too. It's tough losing a friend…"

Jezz swore. "A friend? He'd only been assigned to us this morning. I can't remember if I was even told his name…" He dropped his head into his hands. "I've no idea who he was, why he was here. I don't even know his name, and now he's dead and there's thousands of kids just like him who are going to die fighting these fucking… things…"

Jezz looked up again, his eyes shining and wild.

"We don't even know what they want, why they came here…"

The doctor patted his leg awkwardly.

"I know, son. I know."

Jezz's shoulder slumped. "I haven't even spoken to my family in months. I could be dead so far as they'd know."

The doctor visibly brightened, clearly relieved at having an opening into moving the conversation on.

"Well, that we can take care of."

It had been a while since Jezz had given his family much thought at all. Between the confusion brought about by the phero-induced visions and the fatigue brought on naturally by the dangers and exhaustion of combat, Jezz was very much living one moment to the next. At times, he felt so disconnected that he had started to wonder if he were the hallucination, not the other way around.

He sat in the Comms centre, set up temporarily in an empty school, staring at the monitor in front of him while a lieutenant leaned over his shoulder tapping code furiously into the computer.

Comms, particularly with back home, had been a nightmare for the army. Early into their invasion, the Eltiy'ch had knocked out a swathe of satellites. Between the reduced bandwidth, the prioritisation of military communication, and interference and dropout caused by Eltiy'ch tech, the average soldier had no way of accessing any communication equipment. But the medical corps had argued strongly for the reservation of some equipment so that soldiers suffering from combat-related stress and isolation could be given a small amount of face time with relatives back home, as part of their rehabilitation back to the battlefield. There was no army, they pointed out, if you drove your soldiers to quit, or broke them completely.

The lieutenant stood back. "There you go. You can log onto the videochat now. Fingers crossed you should get five, maybe ten minutes of chat when you get through."

Jezz thanked her, and the woman left him alone. Jezz wearily leaned forward and entered his email address and password. A message came up that told him a connection was being attempted. Then the video window popped up and, after a few seconds of black screen, an image snapped into life. There, looking older and more worn out than Jezz could ever remember seeing him, was his brother.

"Jezz? Oh my God, Jezz, is that you?"

"Hey." Jezz lit a cigarette and gave Keith a tired wave.

"Good grief, it's been months. We've been worried sick…"

"I know, I know. Look, it's not like we get much computer time here, I'm only here now because the doctor thinks…"

"Doctor? Are you wounded, Jezz? Bloody hell, what's…"

Frowning, Jezz slumped down in his chair, coughing. It took a moment for him to recatch his breath, wiping the back of his hand across his mouth. He could still taste that acrid stench of the wounded alien.

"I'm okay, Keith, don't… Look, I'm exhausted, I can't handle the nth degree here. I'm okay, I'm not wounded, I'm not dying. I'm okay. I'm just exhausted and recovering from exposure to an alien hallucinogen…" He waved his hand to cut off his brother's next question. "Just breathe, Keith. It's not… I promise I'm okay. I was exposed, I'm getting a few symptoms but it's not fatal, I'm not in any danger from it. I just need some rest and the doctor thought it'd do me good to get some family time. Speaking of which, where's Dad? Are you at his?"

The connection wasn't great, and the picture therefore not in hi-res, but Jezz could still see his brother whiten. "You didn't get the message?"

"I'm in a combat zone, Keith, no I didn't get the fucking message. Where's Dad?"

"He's in hospital, Jezz. He had a stroke about a month ago. Mum can't look after him now, not how he is at the moment. And I couldn't take him because I had to move in with Mum to look after her."

"And Julia?" Their sister, the accountant.

"Fucking Julia, man, what, you think she'd take him in?"

Jezz looked at his brother for a moment, then shook his head. "I'm sorry, Keith. I'm sorry I'm not there. I should be there."

Keith waved off Jezz's apology. "Nobody's criticising your decision to fight, Jezz. Least of all me. You chose, you all chose, to stand up, to try to hold these things off. If you didn't, what life would there be for any of us?"

Keith looked off camera for a moment.

"Is that Mum?"

"She's asking who I'm talking to."

"Can I speak to her?"

Keith looked cagey. "I don't know, Jezz. She's pretty frail. I don't know if she needs her routine shaking up."

Jezz looked at his brother, biting back an angry retort. It was his fucking mother, and Lord knew Keith and Jezz hadn't seen eye-to-eye in the past, but Jezz didn't have a lot of fight in him right now. Hell, maybe his brother was right. After all, Keith was the one there looking after her. He was at the scene; he knew the score. If she was ill, and knowing how much she loved their dad she would have taken his having a stroke hard, then maybe she didn't need the emotional bombshell of Jezz suddenly turning up, only to disappear again for fuck knows how long.

"Okay, Keith, okay. You're the boss. How are you doing?"

Keith, visibly relieved at Jezz's unexpected compliance, let out a small sigh. "I'm okay, man. Exhausted with looking after Mum, but they've given me time off from the office and Janice is here as well, working from Dad's study. So, that's a help." Keith's wife was not a fan of Jezz, and the feeling was mutual. He decided to gloss over that too.

"That's good you got time off."

"Yeah, but hell, man, what's with you? I mean, you're okay, you said? This chemical thing…? We hear a lot of shit on the news…"

"Yeah, I bet. I mean, fuck, who knows. Could be this will give us all cancer in five years, I dunno. But it's not something people are dying of here. It just… I get these visions."

"Visions?"

"Yeah, like, I lose touch with reality, become…" For a moment, Jezz wanted to pour it all out, his visions of the past, of this other life, but what was the point. Keith would only ask him questions he had no answers to. "I mean, it's nonsense. Hallucinations. It'll wear off. Or it won't. I don't know. But I'm not injured, I'm not hurt. Just out of it. And exhausted."

"You seen them?"

"The Eltiy'ch? Yeah, I've seen them. We're right at the front line here."

"No, I mean, *seen* them. Up close. They say that it's all distant fighting, long range, that you don't get up close."

Jezz grinned, cigarette in mouth, and pulled his t-shirt up to show off his bandages.

"One of them broke my fucking ribs. Hand-to-hand."

"Fuck off!" For a moment, they were teenagers again, two brothers bragging about fights they'd gotten into at school, before adulthood had created a gulf between them.

"No shit. Had to abandon the tank, got in a fistfight with one. Had to stick it to get it off me."

"Shiiiit," Keith's eyes were out on stalks.

"That's time, soldier." A female voice behind him interrupted his story. Jezz waved his hand at her without turning around.

"C'mon, I've only had a few minutes."

"I said that's time, soldier." The lieutenant coughed, a raw hacking cough.

"Keith, man, I've got to go…"

"Yeah, sure, look. I'm really glad you got through Jezz." Something in Keith's voice almost faltered. "It's good to see you."

"You too man." Jezz realised as he spoke how much he actually meant it. "Give my love to Mum and Dad, and Janice too, I guess. And, hey, next time you speak to Julia, tell her to go fuck herself."

"I do, Jezz, regularly."

"Soldier, you need to report back for duty *right now*…" The lieutenant coughed again as she raised her voice angrily, tailing her speech off in a rasping hack.

"Alright! I'm saying goodbye to my fucking brother here…" Jezz turned round, and the cigarette dropped from his mouth to his lap as he stared at the pale blonde in the military uniform behind him.

"Jezz? Jezz! JEZZ!"

8

Jezz woke up, his head spinning. Rolling over, he was promptly sick over the side of the bed. There was no mistaking the oily smell of the Eltiy'ch in his puke. The bedclothes felt exceptionally close on him, as if someone had tucked him in so tight as to stop him escaping. He thrashed at them, the urge to free himself overwhelming.

"Oh shit!" There was a female voice in the room, which was uncomfortably bright. Jezz rolled onto his back and lay there panting, staring at the ceiling. He couldn't see whoever it was who'd sworn when he vomited, but he heard them get up and leave the room. He heard them clatter down a staircase and then more voices. He didn't recognise them, or so he thought at first.

He continued staring at the ceiling. It was white, clean, no cracks or crumbling. If he was in a ward, it wasn't in the field hospital where he'd seen the doctor. Too clean, too quiet. This bed was too comfy. He started to sit up but was overcome by dizziness as soon as he lifted his head off the pillow, so he lay back down again, breathing deeply to stem the sickness.

Had he been shipped out of Ziyang? What had happened? He remembered the doctor saying he'd arrange for him to speak to his family, then the call to Keith. Oh shit, had he been shipped home? Was that Janice who just ran out? He didn't remember ever hearing her curse before, but he had just thrown up all over the floor. Please, God, don't let it be Janice.

He tried sitting up again. By taking it very slowly, he managed to pull himself up so that he was propped up in the bed. The curtains were drawn and there was no light coming in from around them. The light was on in the room, though, so Jezz assumed it was night-time. He didn't recognise the room; it wasn't his parents' house. Tell me this isn't Julia's house. But it didn't look like the sort of pretentious décor he could remember from past video chats with his sister, from before the war. This place looked more… old-fashioned? Sure as hell didn't look Chinese though.

Footsteps on the stairs, less urgent, slower, coming back up. A woman, older than Jezz by at least a couple of decades, appeared in the doorway, the bowl of water in her hands presumably the reason for her more sedate return. There was a whiff of disinfectant. Jezz didn't recognise the woman at all, slightly alarmed by her stick-thin frame and wild, curly shock of hair.

"I'm sorry…" he croaked. His throat was dry, and he coughed. "I'm sorry about your floor."

"It's fine, darling, don't worry. I'm just glad to see you up." There was the hint of an accent; east European, Russian?

She wasn't wearing any kind of uniform.

"Where… where am I?"

She was crouching beside the bed, dabbing the floor with a damp cloth where Jezz had thrown up. At his question, she looked slightly alarmed, though she smothered the expression quickly, as if remembering that she shouldn't worry him. Calmly, but with an undertone, she replied, "You're at home, darling. Well, at mine. We couldn't take you back to the flat."

"They shipped me home? I'm not in a hospital?"

"We wanted you to be, but Doctor Singh couldn't find you a bed. You know what mental health resources are like. Damned Tories. He said as you hadn't done anything dangerous to yourself or others, he couldn't jump you up the list, so I said I'd take you here."

Doctor Singh. The name stirred something in his memory, but Jezz couldn't place it. He shook his head.

The woman stood up and looked down at him, a strange look in her eyes.

"You don't know who I am, do you."

"I'm sorry, I…" Jezz shook his head.

The woman inhaled, as if swallowing back a painful emotion. Then she leant over him and kissed his forehead. "It's okay, darling. Don't worry yourself. Just get some rest."

When he opened his eyes again, it was daytime, and sunlight was streaming in through the open window. Jezz waited a few minutes before trying to sit up, and managed it this time without being sick or feeling dizzy. Same unfamiliar room, but for whatever reason today it felt less… strange, less old-fashioned. He frowned.

He waited a while for someone to appear, but nobody did, so after a while he swung his legs over the side of the bed and braced himself for an attempt to get up. There was a pair of slippers by the side of the bed and a robe over the back of a chair. It almost seemed an open invitation to go exploring.

Stairs, slowly. Living room, spacious. Kitchen. Dining room. This house was larger than any Jezz had ever known, whatever the woman had said about this being 'home', but something about it nagged in the back of his mind. Some echo of familiarity.

He was holding his ribs, still aching from his run-in with the Eltiy'ch. He cricked and rolled his neck, to try and loosen up. Then he opened what looked like a back door leading out onto a terrace.

He stood in the doorway for a moment, hardly believing his senses. He'd braced himself for the cold, having not been able to find anything else to wear, but was shocked to find, in the sunlight, that it was warm. Actually warm. He must be thousands of miles from occupied territory, there wasn't the slightest sign of the aliens' weather manipulation.

"Hey there, sleepy head."

He turned round to see the wild-haired woman reclining on a wooden chair, smoking a cigarette.

"Hey."

"Take a seat, I'll get you breakfast in a minute."

"I'll take one of those first, if you have one."

Jezz winced as he lowered himself into the seat.

"Ribs still hurt, eh? I'm not surprised, when we found you in the shower, we thought you must have cracked a rib or something, the way you fell."

The shower. He'd been in the shower. The girl… the girl had come in. He'd thought it was Sal, but… Sal.

At the recollection of that name, everything flooded back like a tsunami of recovered memory. From out of nowhere, like a burst pipe, Jeff was weeping like a baby. Anya jumped up and had her arms around him in seconds.

"Oh darling, oh my poor darling…"

"I don't want her coming here."

"Jeff, she's really worried about you."

"I get that. But it's pointless. Look at me, I'm a total wreck. It's better for her if she cuts her losses and gets out of this."

Jeff and Anoush were sat in Anya's front room. Jeff in PJs and a bathrobe, wrapped in a blanket, his head recently shaved. He was clutching a cup of tea with both hands. Anoush was in a giraffe onesie, for reasons Jeff couldn't begin to fathom. From the kitchen, there was an intoxicating smell of bacon frying as Anya cooked them breakfast. It was a Saturday morning and both Anya's children were now staying at hers, making her deliriously happy. They could hear her whistling.

Jeff had moved back in. It hadn't taken much, a couple of boxes of clothes, another couple of books, his tv and games console. He'd given up the lease on the flat and taken an extended leave of absence from work. In the end, Anoush and Anya hadn't had to try too hard to persuade him. "You need time, darling," Anya had implored him, hand on his arm. He'd been too tired to argue. If they weren't going to hospitalise him, it was either Anoush's couch for a few months or a bed at Anya's. Comfort won out in the end. Anoush, glad to have a reason not to be alone in her empty flat waiting for Phil to come to his senses, said she'd come back on the weekends too, to help Anya look after Jeff. That was the idea, anyway, although the reality was that Anya, given the chance to mother both of her grown-up children, was now going at full-tilt.

Anoush, her feet up on the sofa and sipping from a glass of orange juice, looked over at Jeff slumped in an armchair. He wasn't wrong, he did look awful. The scruffy beard and shaved head combo was just the starting point. He was getting scarily thin and pale, and his eyes looked like he hadn't slept in a month, despite the fact he was doing little else. That it was taking longer to shake off Jezz when he came to scared him, strengthening the sensation that he was losing his mind. Jeff was trying not to think about the notebook upstairs under his pillow where he had started to amass a detailed sketch of the things he could remember from the hallucinations. If that's what they were. Is it possible that what he was seeing was somehow real? That Jezz really existed, or rather, was going to exist? Jeff didn't believe in premonitions, or never had done, but was this somehow more than just his mind making things up? Some kind of connection through time, maybe. What even was time? He'd never had more than a passing interest in science, but he knew that the idea of time being straightforwardly linear wasn't shared by everyone. Was he somehow *remembering* all this? Jeff stared at a point on the carpet about six feet in front of him as if he was trying to burn a hole in it with his mind. The more he thought about this stuff, the more sick he felt. Part of him felt as if he should be looking into all this online, but a larger part of him felt that that was just the start of a slippery slope towards crackpot conspiracies and tinfoil hats.

Sal had called a few times, even come over once, but Jeff had refused to speak to or see her since coming back to reality the day before. Reality, that was a joke, he thought. Is this reality? Is Jezz reality? Who's the dream here, and who's the one having it? But when he looked up at Anya, entering the room with a tray, he *remembered* this woman, remembered her marrying his dad when his mum died, remembered the years of resentment, remembered her endless forgiveness and kind, kind heart. And Anoush, frustrating, irritating, loving, devoted Anoush. These people were real, here. Look at them! He had lived a whole life as Jeff. Hadn't he?

He took the tray from Anya and the indifference he'd had to the suggestion of breakfast evaporated. Eggs, bacon, a few mushrooms, beans… Fried bread! When was the last time he'd had fried bread? Damn, but it looked amazing. Anya kissed his forehead and took his mug back to the kitchen to refill.

"Smells fabulous, mother!" called Anoush.

"Yours is coming, darling!"

Jeff tucked in and found himself getting hungrier with every bite. Anoush watched him eat, a look of tenderness on her face.

Anya returned with Jeff's tea and a tray for Anoush, then finally again with her own breakfast. She sat on the sofa next to Anoush and turned the tv on. You couldn't have breakfast properly in Anya's house without the BBC. The three sat in silence, half watching the news, munching on their breakfasts.

Jeff took his mug of tea out onto the patio to have with a smoke. Anoush had gone back to her room to catch up on some work, but Anya came with him.

"You don't have to take it in turns to watch me," said Jeff as he lit his cigarette, then leaned over and held the flame up for Anya. He coughed violently, his throat not accustomed to the smoke in the same way his mind appeared to think he was. He mumbled an apology as he leant over the side of his seat and spat onto the patio.

"Hush, darling, we don't need paranoia on top of psychosis." She leaned back in her chair and exhaled, ignoring the dour look Jeff shot at her. "What are your plans for today?"

"I'm not seeing Sal, if that's what you're asking."

Anya waved her hand, dismissing the idea. "No, no, I wasn't asking that. I just meant what are you doing? You can't stay in your pyjamas all day."

"I can't?"

"No, darling. I invited you here so I could take care of you, not to watch you turn into a bum. When you've had your tea, you can go upstairs and get dressed, please. Then we can think of something for you to do."

They sat for a moment, watching squirrels helping themselves to the contents of a bird feeder.

"I haven't seen the sea for a while," Jeff said quietly, half to himself.

"Darling, what a splendid idea! I have a lesson in a bit, but after that we could put a picnic together and drive out to the coast. It's supposed to stay dry today."

"Teaching on a Saturday now?"

Anya shook her head. "No, no, it's just that Sophie has an exam coming up. She could do with a few extra lessons, just to sharpen her up."

Jeff nodded and took another sip of his tea. "Bit cold for the beach, isn't it?"

"Nonsense, it'll be bracing. Good for you. Clear the mind."

"I wish."

Anya laughed and dropped her cigarette into the empty plant pot she kept between the chairs. She got up, kissed Jeff on the top of his head, patted his arm and headed inside. "Don't stay out here too long, darling. I want you decent when Sophie arrives."

"Decent? I am decent. I'm practically mummified in this blanket."

It would be nice to get out though, he realised. His instincts were to go back to bed, pull the duvet over his head and try to go back to sleep, but Jeff knew that wouldn't be conducive to sorting his head out. He may be exhausted, but he needed regular sleep patterns, not sleeping every chance he got. So he got dressed; jeans, t-shirt, long-sleeve, hoodie, and trainers. He picked a book up off the shelf in his room without looking at it and went downstairs.

He slumped into a chair in the front room and was almost instantly hustled out again by Anya. "Not in here, darling, it's where I teach. Why don't you go to the study?"

He sighed and dragged himself down the hallway to the closed door at the far end. He felt a touch of trepidation at the door. This room had been his father's space, and Jeff hadn't set foot in it more than a couple of times in the years since his death. Jeff could feel his presence in the entire house, of course, but this room in particular had been Jack's and Jack's alone. It would, in all honesty, have made a better room for Anya to teach in, had she not been alone in the whole house for years anyway. But Jeff knew that even had she not lived alone, she would have been as superstitious about this room as Jeff was, and that she would have done anything to leave it undisturbed.

He steeled himself and entered. It was exactly how his father had left it, other than the desk which had at least been tidied. But the bookshelves were his, the desk still had his computer - *I mean, honestly, there's no way that thing can still work, is there?* - and stationery on it. A picture of Jack and Anya also stood on the desk, and hanging on the wall above the sofa that Jack used to read on was a picture of Jack, Jeff and Melissa, Jeff's mother. Jeff was very young in the photo, maybe three or four. The three of them were posing on a beach. It looked hot and all three of them were in swimming costumes. Spain, Jack had told him, though Jeff had no memory of the holiday.

He stared at the photo for a few minutes, aching in his heart at the sight of his mother, younger than Jeff was now, not knowing that a couple of years after this photo was taken, she would be diagnosed with the cancer that would kill her. Jeff's instinct to reach a hand up and touch the picture, but that made him feel clichéd and mawkish. Instead, he flopped down on the sofa and finally looked at the book he'd picked up to see what it was.

"Hmm," Jeff said to himself, "I don't think so." There was a woman on the cover, in a floaty dress, stood on a hilltop with a man whose shirt was unbuttoned to the waist. His stepmother, somewhat of an intellectual, had surprisingly horrible taste in fiction. His father's shelves, however, were more fruitful. Jeff picked out a Somerset Maugham and settled in for the morning.

A knock at the door brought Jeff out of Philip Carey's life and back to the present.

"Do you want a tea?" It was Anoush. "Mother's just finishing up."

"Okay, sure."

Jeff grabbed a piece of scrap paper from the desk, tore off a strip and inserted it into the book to mark his place. Then, leaving the book on the sofa, he left the study and went through to the kitchen.

Anoush was putting the kettle on, so Jeff took three mugs down from the shelf and looked around for the tea caddy.

"Four."

"Hmm?"

"Four cups, Sophie's having one."

"Sure," Jeff grabbed a fourth and then, finding the jar, dropped a teabag into each.

Anoush had gone back to the chopping board where she was making sandwiches. "Cheese okay?"

"Fine."

The kettle boiled and Jeff poured out four cups. He went to the fridge for milk, noticing for the first time that Anoush was wrapping up the sandwiches and putting them in a large bag on the counter.

"We're really doing this?"

"Your idea, shithead. I'm supposed to be finishing a report this afternoon."

"We don't have to…"

Anoush waved her hand at him. "It's fine, I'm getting nowhere anyway. Maybe this is what I need. It's just a few hours, I can come back, finish it and still be done in time to watch a movie with you guys this evening."

"We're settling into a routine, huh."

Anoush slid past him, reaching up to a cupboard and pulling out some crisps. She kissed his cheek on the way back. "I'm sorry, babes, did you have plans?"

Jeff scowled at her and stepped outside.

Anya's tired and somewhat filthy Fiesta drew up into the car park. There weren't that many cars about, though frankly with the way the wind had got up, Jeff was surprised there was many as there were. He let himself out of the backseat and almost instantly cursed as the wind cut through him. He zipped up Anya's fleece that he'd borrowed and pulled his hat down tight.

Anoush, in the front passenger seat, got out and had a similar reaction. "For shit's sake. This is ridiculous."

"Nonsense, darling, this will clear your mind, clear your lungs. An hour of this and you'll feel a new person."

Anya and Sophie were getting out of the other side of the vehicle. The teenager was the least appropriately dressed of any of them, having only decided to come along when Anya, on a whim, asked her if she'd like to. She had nothing else to do, it transpired, and now stood in leggings and a hoodie, limp red hair whipping round her face.

"Sophie, you'll freeze out here," said Anoush, frowning at the girl.

"I'm alright."

Anya grabbed her around the shoulders, "Of course you are, darling, teenagers don't feel the cold. Come on, let's get going. Are we taking the picnic?"

"Don't be absurd, mother. We can have it in the car when we get back. I'm not sitting down on the beach in this."

Anya conceded the point, and the four of them set off. The car park was an open grassy field, with a Pay Machine and a notice declaring the first two hours to be free.

"Do we..."

"No!" chorused Jeff and Anoush, trudging ahead towards the dunes. Sophie giggled, cuddling up to Anya as they followed.

It was cold, yes, and windy, but the sun was shining. As they crested the dune and caught their first sight of the sea, Jeff stood for a moment, drinking the sight in. The tide was in, so there was not much beach to be seen, the waves crashing about fifty feet from where the dunes rolled down. It was beautiful, and as much as he hated to admit it, Anya was right. He already felt better. Better for being out of the house, better for the fresh air. Better for the freezing cold even, making him feel more alive and shaking him out of his stupor.

Anoush pushed him and the two of them started racing down the dune.

The four of them wandered slowly along the beach, every now and then one of them bending to look at something or stopping to take a photo on their phone. Anya made Sophie take a picture of the four of them looking windswept and huddling together, grinning cheesily and generally mugging, then insisted the poor girl post it on her Instagram, at which Jeff and Anoush shared a look.

Anoush was arm-in-arm with her mother now, just ahead of where Jeff was walking with Sophie. She had tied her hair, which was as dank and lifeless as Jeff remembered, back now, although stray strands were still whipping round her face, causing her to reach up and try to tuck them behind her ear every few minutes.

"So, you're living at Mrs Ginetti's now? How come?"

Jeff, his hands buried as deep as he could get them in the pockets of Anya's fleece, thought about making something up, but the kid looked reasonably sensible. He glanced up at Anya to see if she'd heard the question, but if she had she was ignoring it.

"I'm not very well."

"I'm sorry. What's wrong?"

"Head stuff. I guess I'm having a breakdown."

Sophie nodded. "I figured. You look like shit compared to when I last met you."

"Thanks."

"It's okay, we're all carrying shit." Sophie rolled up the sleeves of her hoodie to reveal her heavily freckled arms. Faint scars criss-crossed her wrists.

"Bloody hell."

Sophie shrugged as she rolled the sleeves down again. "They're old. I haven't done it for a couple of years. But I get it. I'm not scared of talking about that sort of thing."

Jeff tried to cover the awkwardness he was feeling by crouching down and examining a shell that caught his eye. Sophie carried on, oblivious.

"Half the kids in my class are on some kind of meds."

"I see things." Jeff blurted out, standing up and starting to walk again.

"Like, dead people?"

"Ha-ha. No, I mean I have hallucinations, prolonged ones. Completely immersive, where I feel I'm someone else living a different life."

"Oh. Wild."

Anoush and Anya were a little way ahead now, and Jeff suddenly felt a little anxious about having this conversation with a teenager. Anoush looked back over her shoulder and waved at them.

"Come on, we should catch up."

"You don't like talking about it."

"Not especially, no."

"Okay. That's cool."

They started walking a bit faster and were soon with Anya and Anoush again. Jeff pretended he didn't notice the way Sophie was looking at him.

They sat in the car and ate their sandwiches. Jeff had called shotgun, so Anoush was sitting in the back with Sophie. He was slightly more at ease now the girl was further away from him.

"There," said Anya, through a mouthful of lettuce and cheese, "doesn't everyone feel better for that?"

"It was bracing, I'll give you that," conceded Jeff.

"It was lovely, mother. I do so enjoy freezing my tits off."

"I enjoyed it, Mrs Ginetti. It was nice to see the sea."

"It's Anya, darling, we're not in a lesson now."

Anoush, now sitting next to the picnic bag, took out a couple of chocolate bars and passed them forward. Jeff took his and put it on the dashboard, pulling a cigarette out of his pocket instead. "I'm just stepping outside."

Anya reached out her hand and Jeff passed her one. The pair of them got out. Jeff walked round and perched on the front of the car, lighting his cigarette under the cover of his fleece.

"I'm sorry, darling, was Sophie interrogating you?"

"It's okay."

"She's a good kid. Not much of a home life, that's why I asked her along."

"You know she self-harms?"

"She used to, darling. She was in bandages quite often when she came to lessons, a year or so ago. She's much better now her father moved out."

"She's a bit intense."

"I should have thought, young handsome man like you," said Anya, rubbing a hand over her stepson's scalp. "Probably wasn't a good idea of mine to bring her along. I hope she's not forming a crush."

"It's fine. One afternoon isn't going to hurt."

"And you? How are you?"

"I'm okay. You were right, this was a good idea. I feel more with it now. The cold air certainly seems to have woken me up."

The car horn sounded, making them jump. Turning around, they saw Anoush leaning over the front seat, banging the steering wheel. She pointed at her watch.

"What's her hurry?"

"I think she wanted to get back and do some work this afternoon."

"That girl works too hard."

They dropped Sophie off at her mum's on the way back home, and she stood on the front step to wave them off, before turning around and going inside.

"Someone's got a new member of his fanclub."

"Shut up, Anoush." Jeff slumped down in the front seat, his eyes closed. "Just leave it, eh?"

"Come on, darlings, it's been a nice day, don't ruin it."

It was a brief journey back to Anya's from Sophie's. They drove the rest of the way in silence.

Jeff was almost asleep in the front when they pulled in, so for a moment didn't register the significance of Anya's "Oh dear" as they drove up to the front door. Then he saw the blonde figure sitting on the front step, huddled up in a long, thick coat.

It was Sal.

They sat out on the patio, Anya bringing them hot chocolate and a couple of blankets, then discreetly retreating. Sal sipped timidly at her drink, perched on the very front of one of Anya's Adirondack chairs, blanket around her shoulders. Jeff sunk into his chair, blanket over his legs, and lit a cigarette.

Neither of them looked at the other.

"I'm glad you came," said Jeff, after a while.

"You are? I didn't think you would be."

"Why wouldn't I be?"

"Erm, you refused to talk to me or see me?" Sal's tone was reserved, calm. She clearly hadn't come for a fight, but equally clearly wasn't sure where this was likely to end up.

Jeff took a drag on his cigarette, exhaled, then rubbed a hand over his tired face. He dropped the half-smoked cigarette into the flowerpot. It was making his mouth taste horrible.

"It's just, look, I didn't want you to come because… I didn't want you to get sucked in, or feel you were obliged to or anything. I was worried you'd come because you felt it was expected. Let's face it, we've only just met, we're not even… We were just seeing where we were. You met me at a very strange time in my life."

"I know, you quoted that at me before."

"It's not that I didn't want to see you. I really wanted to see you. But it just felt terribly unfair to expect you to deal with any of this. We'd just met, you seem great, we liked each other, but if you went now, it would just be this thing where you met a guy, but nothing came of it. In a couple of months' time, you wouldn't really think much of it. Whereas you stick around, and I don't know how this goes, how much worse this gets."

Sal sipped again at her drink, and they were silent for a while. A jay flew down onto the fence halfway down the garden. They watched it as it looked around and then flew off again.

"This is all pretty messed up, is all I'm saying."

"I know," Sal took a deep breath, "and if I'm honest, part of me was relieved when you said you didn't want to speak to me." She was looking down at her tea, as if the admission had shamed her. "You're obviously going through something serious that I don't know the first thing about and feel totally ill-equipped to deal with. If I'm being truthful, I was glad I had an out."

"So, what changed?"

Sal shrugged. "I realised I didn't want to take it."

"You don't owe me anything…"

"Shut up, Jeff, and listen. I'm not here because I feel I ought to be. I'm here because I didn't want to not be."

"You didn't not want to be?"

"I didn't not want not to not be?" Sal giggled to herself, though it was still a soft, unsure giggle. She looked up at him, green eyes glistening, seemingly moments away from tears. "I really like you. I didn't like the thought of not seeing you again."

She held out her hand to Jeff. After a moment, he reached over and took it in his.

They stayed that way for a long while.

The four of them were bunched up on the sofa which, though technically big enough for four, was a bit of a stretch once blankets and bowls of popcorn were thrown into the mix. But Anoush had been insistent. "Pyjamas, all of you, onesies, whatever. Blankets, popcorn, all on the sofa. We do this properly or not at all. I've spent the last two hours writing this damned report and now I want to snuggle up and watch a movie."

So, there they sat. Anya, Jeff, Sal and Anoush, blankets over their laps and two large snack bowls balanced precariously on their collective laps. They'd let Jeff pick a movie, then unanimously shouted down his choice and were instead watching one of Anoush's less-taxing favourites. Anya had her arm around her stepson, Sal snuggled in under his arm in turn, while Anoush had her legs up across their three laps.

Jeff couldn't remember the last time he felt this safe, and it wasn't long before he drifted off, as indifferent as he was to the outcome of Sandra Bullock and Ryan Reynolds' relationship.

When the film reached its conclusion and Anya and Anoush were in floods, the group slowly extricated themselves from each other's limbs. Anya invited Sal to stay the night, she declined, Anoush insisted and then she accepted.

"Do you want me to put a bed together...?"

Sal, blushing slightly, looked down at Jeff who was rubbing his eyes as he woke himself up just enough to manage the stairs. "No, erm, if it's okay, I can just..."

Anya leaned over and kissed her on the forehead. "Of course, darling."

Anoush punched Jeff on the arm. "Goodnight, everyone."

And for Jeff, it was.

Daylight streamed in through a crack in the curtains and found Jeff lying in bed, his arm around Sal, feeling the most relaxed he had upon waking for most of that year. In the back of his mind, there were concerns, of course. About when the next episode might happen, about whether Sal would regret her decision, about whether they would end up hurting each other, about whether he'd end up falling for her and what that meant, about the future in general. But as he looked down at her, still dozing, he felt a surge of warmth go through his body and realised that, on one count at least, it was already too late to be worried about what-ifs.

The morning passed quietly, as Sunday mornings have a wont to do. Anya made porridge as the family slowly assembled downstairs, and a plan was made to go out for lunch, get a roast somewhere. Sal, after a discussion with Anya and Anoush, agreed to stay that night as well, so left to go pick up some things. Jeff went to the study and picked up the Somerset Maugham for a couple of hours.

There was a moment late in the morning when Jeff's heart froze at the sound of a helicopter, but it passed quickly. A casual enquiry as he went through the kitchen on his way to the patio for a smoke confirmed that it had actually happened, one had passed overhead. "Probably one of your buddies escaped from the hospital," said Anoush. "Happens every now and then."

Out on the patio, Anya was sitting smoking and reading under a blanket. She held up her hand to Jeff as walked behind her to the other seat, squeezing his as he gave it. She slowly turned the page as he sat down, finished her chapter, then to Jeff's horror folded the corner of the page down. She put her book down on the patio beside her chair and removed her glasses.

"How are you, darling?"

"I'm okay. I don't feel so tired today."

Anya smiled at him, tenderly. "She's a lovely girl."

"She is that."

"I'm glad, darling, you need some love in your life."

"Well, let's not get carried away."

"You know what I mean. Some warmth, some companionship. You've been alone in that flat for too long."

"Maybe you're right," said Jeff, rubbing his scalp.

"Trust me, darling, your wicked old stepmother is always right."

Jeff reached out a hand to her. "Thank you."

Anya squeezed his hand. "You are always welcome, Jeffrey."

"You've been so very good to me."

"You're my son. When I married your father, I married his family. That's the deal. You don't ignore a child just because you didn't bear it, not when you make that commitment. And besides, I loved that man to death, darling, you know that. How could I ever look him in the eye if I didn't take care of you now he's gone?"

"You're a good woman. I'm sorry it took me so long to realise it."

"Oh hush, darling, you'll make me weep, and my eyes haven't recovered from that damned film yet."

They sat there for a few moments in silence, until Jeff finally said, "I'm worried about Sal."

"What do you mean?"

"Taking me on. It doesn't seem like the sensible thing for her to do. Would she be better off just walking away before we got too involved?"

"Maybe she would."

Anya's honest response took Jeff by surprise. "You seemed pretty keen on her staying last night."

"And I was. Because I could see she wanted to. Darling, that girl is crazy about you, more than even she knows. And it may well be that she'll end up hurt because of that. But that's what love is, the potential for pain. No, the certainty of pain. But what's the alternative? Besides," Anya shrugged and lit a cigarette for herself, "she's a grown woman. You are going to make that choice for her?"

Jeff didn't respond straight away.

"If you don't hurt her, someone else will. If she doesn't hurt you, someone else will. Being with someone is just about choosing who's going to hurt you someday. Who it's worth being hurt for. And, my darling, I happen to know that she could do a lot worse than be hurt by you."

Jeff laughed. "Thanks."

"My God, is he laughing? How did you manage that?" asked Anoush, coming out onto the patio. "I had forgotten what that sounds like."

"Well maybe if you made me watch more romantic 'comedies' that were actually funny, you'd hear it more often."

Anoush stuck her tongue out at him.

"I'm putting the kettle on. If you two are done giving yourself cancer, do you want one?"

Jeff and Anya both raised their hands.

Jeff stretched as he got out of Anya's dilapidated Fiesta in the pub car park. As soon as Sal had returned, the four of them had left to get their roast dinner. Sal gave Jeff a quick squeeze then headed inside with Anoush. Anya was still sat in the driver's seat, texting someone, both thumbs banging away. Jeff lit a cigarette and went to huddle on one of the unused benches in the pub garden.

He waved at Anya when she finally got out, and mimed offering her a cigarette, but she just waved back and headed in after the others. Jeff swung his legs around over the bench and rested his elbows on the table. For a few minutes, he watched a squirrel running back and forth along the fence to the garden.

Stubbing out his cigarette, Jeff swivelled round, stood up, and froze. On the far side of the car park stood a slender woman in a long black coat. She had a beret on, covering her eyes as she held her head low, but Jeff could see the telltale almost white hair beneath.

His heart pounding in his chest, he wondered what to do. If he got into the pub and back with the others, could he avoid the episode? Or at least delay it, as he had last time? On the other hand, was it time to face it down? He concentrated on his breathing, in through the nose, not deep breaths but slow ones.

The woman hadn't moved but was definitely waiting for him. Any doubt in his mind that this might just be an actual woman who happened to be in the car park looking at him evaporated as she raised an impossibly pale hand to him and beckoned him.

Almost against his will, he found himself approaching her.

"This is not what you think it is."

"To be honest, I'm getting really fed up with you saying that."

He was close now, just a few feet away, but the woman was still looking down, preventing Jeff from seeing most of her face. Jeff was starting to assume there wasn't one, though he could make out her mouth as she spoke again, "We can't continue as we are."

"Well, on that we agree."

"We need to make a choice."

"We… what?"

The pale woman raised a hand to her mouth, for a moment overcome by a coughing fit. Jeff looked away as she spat on the ground, wiping the back of her hand across her mouth.

"That's a nasty cough you have there, you ought to get that looked at."

"We need to make a choice," she continued, ignoring his remark.

"I don't understand. What choice?"

"I can't do this for myself, Jeff." It almost sounded to Jeff as if she was scared. *She* was scared?

"Look, if you want something from me, you need to tell me what. This cryptic stuff… None of this is making any sense to me…"

He reached out to grab her arm, but as he did so, he heard Sal calling him from the pub door. In the moment it took to react to that, then turn back to the pale woman, she was gone.

Sal came up beside him. "Jeff, what is it?"

"She… she was here."

Sal grabbed for him as he started to sway, and his knees buckled.

"It's okay, baby, it's okay. I'm here, I'm here…"

The restorative powers of a roast dinner are not to be taken lightly. Sal, talking softly but constantly had managed to keep Jeff with her even as his legs gave way and he sat down in the car park. She gave an irritated wave to the driver of the SUV who beeped and stared down at them as he entered the car park, continuing to engage Jeff's attention until he felt strong enough to stand up again. By then, Anoush had appeared to find out what had happened to them. Between them, the two women helped him into the pub and to their table.

He fell to his dinner with a vigour that surprised the others and indeed, it wasn't long before he was joining in with their chatter, which grew less concerned as he seemed to come back to life. Jeff was well aware of the looks the three of them were still occasionally giving him, and each other, but of course he understood why, so didn't draw attention to it.

The pub was locally renowned for its carvery and Jeff had piled his plate high, but even so he made short work of it, ordering a dessert as well. His appetite had been sporadic at best, for some months, but now he decided that maybe he needed to force himself to bring his strength up. Maybe that was why he'd been passing out and having these visions. The depression and feeling of being strung out had left him weak, and… Anyway, this carvery was bloody good.

He knocked back the rest of his non-alcoholic beer and leant back in his seat, feeling full and satisfied. Sal rested a hand on his leg.

"You okay, babes?" asked Anoush.

Jeff nodded, "I think so. Yeah, maybe I was just hungry." He hadn't mentioned the pale woman to anyone except Sal and decided in that moment, that if he had sidestepped an episode, he'd keep it that way.

"You want to head home? Or maybe walk some of this off?" Anya often suggested a Sunday afternoon walk, usually to no avail. So she was grateful when Sal was keen to take up the idea.

"Sure, that'd be nice. We could go up to the heath, have an hour or two out. Jeff?"

"Yeah, I guess. Okay."

Anoush shrugged, "Sure, why not."

They paid and left, taking the five-minute drive to one of the car parks around the heath, and set off on their walk. Jeff walked arm-in-arm with Sal and, casually, they let the other two start to get ahead.

"Are you okay?" Sal's tone indicated that this wasn't a casual question.

"Yep. I'm better, feeling better. Still wary, but for sure, the food helped. And I don't seem to see her when I'm with others, so as long as you don't run off anywhere, I should be okay."

She leaned up and kissed him on the cheek, then pulled him to a stop and gave him another, longer kiss on the mouth.

As they parted, Jeff glanced to where Anya and Anoush had gone, just in time to see them disappear.

"We'd better catch them up."

Sal gave him a sly grin. "Had we?"

Jeff raised his eyebrows and allowed her to pull him off the path.

It was called the heath, but it was more woodland than heathland. In this part, in particular, you didn't have to stray far from the path to reach a spot where you couldn't be seen from it. Sal giggled as she pulled at Jeff's arm, then pushed him up against a tree and kissed him again, pressing her body against his.

They kissed deeply, making Jeff's heart start to race. He held her in his arms, almost lifting her off her feet, then gasped as she ran her hand down his chest and over his crotch. His body reacted instantly, and Sal's eyes shone as she broke away from him for a moment. She gave him a mischievous grin.

"Someone's enjoying themselves."

He pulled her back and kissed her again, lowering his hand and softly squeezing her breast as she tugged at his belt. Her hand was cold and he almost yelped as she slipped it down inside the waistband of his underwear. She was moaning softly as she kissed him now, her nipple hardening enough for him to feel it through the fabric of her jumper. She took a firm hold of him and started to stroke…

"We thought you'd gotten lost."

Anya looked slightly concerned as Jeff and Sal caught them up at one of the picnic spots where she and Anoush had stopped to wait for them.

"Sorry, we got to talking," said Sal. "Didn't realise how far we'd dropped back."

Over Anya's shoulder, Jeff could see Anoush grinning wolfishly and had to stop himself from sticking his fingers up at her. Instead, he said, "Come on, let's get back to the car. I could do with a kip."

"I bet you could," muttered Anoush.

"What was that, darling?"

"Nothing, mother. Come on, Jeff's right, it's getting cold, we should get back and get a fire started." She made a point of putting her arm in Sal's and striding off.

Another evening spent wrapped up with his family on the couch, another mediocre movie enjoyed in comfort and safety, another good night's sleep. Jeff and Sal didn't make love, but the warmth of her body next to his was a source of tremendous joy to Jeff, and he felt himself relax in the security of her presence.

The next morning, she kissed him sleepily and went off to shower. Monday meant work, for Sal at least, and Jeff felt surprisingly uncomfortable at the idea of spending the day without her. But Anya worked from home so he wouldn't be on his own. He could relax with the Maugham while he waited for Sal to return, that was okay.

He contemplated lying in bed for a while but felt invigorated enough by his weekend that the urge to pull the covers up and go back to sleep was hardly there, so instead, rubbing his scalp, he yawned and sat up. There wasn't much daylight coming through the curtains, it was still early. Maybe he could get up and make breakfast for everyone. So refreshed was he feeling that he didn't even register how uncharacteristic a thought that was.

Swinging his legs out over the bed, he got up, stretched and walked over to the window. He pulled open the curtains and recoiled in horror.

Outside, an unfamiliar city spread out before him, smoke curling up between old tower blocks, and the chatter of gunfire could be heard from the direction of the river that bent and twisted in the distance. There was a dim, reddish glow off to the left where a fire was raging. In the nearest streets, figures could be made out, running, and armoured vehicles were slowly driving along the main thoroughfare that stretched out before the window. One of them, close by, fired a shell from its main gun, the boom reverberating in the manmade canyons of the built-up city streets.

Jeff stumbled back, making only a couple of steps before tripping and falling. His heart pounding, he lay on the floor, breathing racing out of control.

"What are you planning… Jeff!"

Sal ran in, clutching her towel to herself with one hand and reaching out to him with the other. She knelt beside him, her face contorted by fear and concern. "Jeff, hon, what is it?"

He pointed at the window, unable to speak.

Sal stood up and looked, "What is it, honey? What am I looking for? Did you see her again?"

Slowly, Jeff managed to get to his feet and stood beside her, looking out of the window at Anya's garden in the early morning light.

"I can call in, I've got some leave left."

"No, it's fine, really. Anya's here, I won't be on my own."

"I'm not going anywhere today, darling," said Anya, reassuringly. "We'll both be here when you get home."

The three of them were on the patio, Jeff and Anya wrapped up in blankets on the chairs, with tea and cigarettes. Sal stood, her bag slung over her shoulder, ready but reluctant to leave.

Jeff put his cigarette in his mouth, squinting at the smoke curling up into his eye, and reached a spare hand out to her. She took it, the concern apparent in her eyes. "I'll be okay." He tried to fill his voice with reassurance. "I had a moment, it passed, everything's fine. Go to work."

"If you're sure… I could do with swinging by home, picking up a few things. You're sure it's okay for me to stay here for a few nights?" The question was to Anya.

"Darling, stay as long as you want. It's lovely having the house full of young people again."

"Well, okay," Sal still didn't look convinced, but she squeezed Jeff's hand and let it go. Bending over to give Anya the kiss that she clearly expected, Sal gave them a tentative wave and left round the corner of the house. They heard her footsteps on the gravel drive, listening to her until she was gone.

"Thank you."

"Oh hush, darling, I adore her already, I love having her here. She brightens the place up, and with you here, God knows it could do with it." Anya winked at him.

Jeff gave her a strained smile.

He couldn't focus on his book, and he ended up spending the morning idly thumbing his phone, jumping from one social media platform to another, half-reading articles and seeing what his friends, who he rarely spoke to, had been doing recently. He spent half an hour playing a game whose ad had caught his eye, before crashing up against the need for in-game purchases. That was when he put the phone on the floor beside the couch he was lying on and took out the notebook he'd been trying to record the hallucinations in.

The city, had that been Ziyang? He'd noted something down about tanks, a river. He picked up the phone again and looked up Ziyang. It was a real place; and had a river. He spent a fruitless ten minutes trying to see if any of the pictures he could find online bore any resemblance to the war-torn city he'd seen from his bedroom window. Well, it could have been, he thought. The buildings are… Buildings. He shook his head, this was pointless, he was crazy to think… Wait! No… Giora growled in annoyance as Jeff sat up, dislodging the cat from where it had been relaxing on his stomach.

One building, a tower block with an advertising hoarding up the side; for some reason the view of it on his phone sent a flash of recognition through his brain. Had that been in the vision?

He dropped the phone and started to lose control of his breathing again. The room swam as he shook his head violently to try and clear it.

This was nuts. How had he seen a real city out of the window this morning? He'd never heard of Ziyang before this all started. He'd had to look it up to see if it was even a real place. What the *hell*?

Jeff focused on slowing his breathing. Look, he reasoned, it's a building. With an advertising hoarding. Big deal, there must be millions of them in China, and they probably all look very similar. Or maybe his brain had dredged it up from some film or documentary he'd watched. Hell, it could have been in the background of some Instagram post he'd seen. Didn't Chloe go travelling in China a few years back? Maybe he should ask her if she ever visited Ziyang.

Yeah, sure, explain *that* sudden interest.

Jeff lay on the couch for a while, staring at the ceiling, deeply troubled by this disturbing development.

In the end, abandoning any idea of getting anything done at Anya's, he decided to take a walk into town. Anya wasn't wild about the idea, he could tell, but he waved off her concerns and to her credit, she didn't make a fuss. Reassuring her that he had his phone on him and that he'd call her if anything happened, he threw on a coat and left.

He had no plan, so after the twenty minutes it took to get into the centre of town, he just wandered. He went into Waterstones and checked out books on China, but there was nothing that really gave him much on Ziyang. And anyway, he figured he could get what he needed from the internet, if he could even identify what it was that he was after. So instead, he mooched, eventually finding himself near the coffee shop where he had first seen the pale woman. He looked around with some trepidation, but there was no sign of anything untoward. He cast an uncertain eye at the independent book shop across the road, but there was no sign of her there either.

"Pull yourself together," he muttered as he entered the coffee shop. An old woman who was just leaving glared at him and it took him a moment to realise that she thought he was muttering at her. He offered her a meek apology. Ordering a drink, he took a seat at the window. The outside seating hadn't been put out, presumably that was over until spring.

Jeff sat looking out on the street. He sipped occasionally at his hot chocolate but didn't really taste it. He felt disconcerted, disconnected. He could see people passing outside and they looked normal enough, but the whole thing felt unreal, like he was watching a film.

He wasn't surprised when he saw her. The disconnect had been mounting since he'd seen her in the car park at the pub the day before, and he was in no doubt that sooner or later she would reappear. He cursed himself for his stupidity, for being outside in the world. At least at Anya's he would have… what? Passed out in the shower again? On the sofa? They could have put him to bed, let him sleep it off, but now, out here, what would happen?

She stood by the book shop window, facing him, but again with her head tilted down in such a way as to prevent him really seeing her face. He knew she was watching him though, looking somehow straight at him. He drained his hot chocolate, in half a mind to stay where he was, to force her, it, to come to him. But somehow, he knew that that wasn't how this was going to play out. Putting on his coat, he left the coffee shop and strode across the street.

He never even saw the cyclist.

9

Dammit, that hurt. Jeff woke up bruised and aching. His arm and shoulder were on fire, and his ribs, still smarting from the fall in the shower, were really painful too. As he went to sit up, he let out an involuntary bark of pain, which in turn was swiftly cut off by a choking cough. He leaned over the side of the bed and hawked up what felt like a lungful of thick, oily gloop.

At the noise, a nurse walked swiftly into the room. A nurse? Shit, so he was back in hospital. The sheets were rough, though, and this bed was… where the hell was he? His eyes darted from side to side as he took in the surprisingly small room. It was like he'd been put in a closet…

"You're awake, that's good. No, don't try and move, you'll need another six hours or so for the ReadiSet to finish working."

The…. What? "Where, where am I?"

"You don't remember?" Frowning, the nurse grabbed the chart from the bottom of his bed and gave it a quick once over, murmuring to himself. "Hmm, no head injuries, you shouldn't… oh wait, no, there's a phero exposure from a few weeks ago." The nurse looked up. "Shouldn't still be affecting you, but that must be it."

What on earth was he talking about?

"I don't understand what you're saying to me."

The nurse returned the chart to its place on the bed and walked around to stand beside him, reaching down to wave some kind of gadget at his forehead.

"You took a nasty fall in the comms centre, caught your foot as you were trying to get up. You fell awkwardly onto one of the tables. Made quite the mess of your arm, at that. Which wouldn't have been so bad, but we think you were lying there for a couple of hours before anyone found you."

"I wasn't in any comms centre… I was getting a coffee, in town. What the hell is going on here?"

The nurse frowned again, and this time looked him straight in the eye, for the first time since he came into the room.

"You really don't remember where you are?"

"I *remember* exactly where I was, I don't *know* where I am."

"I'll get Doctor Ross to come in and examine you."

"Doctor Ross? I don't know a Doctor Ross. Is Doctor Singh not here?"

"We've no India Corps personnel in this sector, I don't know anything about your Doctor Singh. Doctor Ross will be here in a minute." And with that, the nurse left.

Slowly, gingerly, Jeff tried again to sit up; this time making it with only a slight yelp. There were no slippers under the bed. It wasn't even really a bed, just a trolley. Wherever he was, this was not any hospital he recognised. He tried standing. When the dizziness and nausea passed, he tried standing again. On the third attempt, he made it to his feet.

Leaning heavily against the door frame, he looked out into what turned out to be a large room. It seemed as if he'd been put in a small side room adjacent to a much larger ward. Ten beds, each occupied, were arrayed in what could charitably be described as just enough space. The men in the beds seemed to have a variety of injuries... Jeff frowned, yep, they were all injuries. Clearly no one was here for any kind of sickness, this wasn't a general ward. Everyone seemed to be suffering from some kind of major injury. Limbs plastered and bandaged, heads too, in a few cases. And the bandages weren't what Jeff would call clean, either. It looked like a hospital on the news, in a piece from a war zone...

"Oh fuck!" Jeff, relying heavily on the wall for support, made his way over to the window and with horror looked out on a war-torn city. Smoke, the distant sound of gunfire, a dim reddish glow off to the left and a river in the distance, soldiers on the streets below...

"Ziyang..." How was *he* here? This was wrong, so very wrong...

"Where else did you think you were?" asked the soldier in the bed Jeff was standing next to. "Paris?" The soldier laughed at his own joke. Jeff was astonished to realise that the soldier was smoking.

"Can I... can I have one of those?"

The soldier offered up his pack wordlessly, then his lighter. Jeff, inhaling deeply, started to cough.

"Yeah, sorry, Chinese. I haven't seen a decent cigarette in weeks."

Jeff waved his hand at the soldier. "It's fine."

He felt woozy though, and the cigarette hadn't helped. What was he doing here? What was *he* doing here?

He backed away from the window. This is a nightmare, it must be, I don't know what's happening to me...

"Jezz!"

At the sound of almost his name, Jeff looked up and saw a big bear of a man standing in the main door to the ward.

"Teemu?"

"Jezz!" The man called again, and then lumbered towards him, arms outstretched.

"Teemu!" Jezz shuddered, a jerking sensation running through his entire body, as if reality just slipped a gear. He promptly threw up.

"For fuck's sake," he heard the soldier who'd given him the cigarette curse. It's a good job he can't see I just pissed myself too, thought Jezz.

"Can you get me paper? And a pen."

"Sure Jezz, but take it easy, man, that doctor said you need rest."

"I need to write this shit down, Teemu, now. While it's still fresh in my head."

Jezz was back in bed now, in a clean gown. Teemu had picked him up and carried him back to his room, then called for the nurse. Clearly the nurse had better things he thought he should be doing, as, along with fresh clothes, he brought a lecture about moving about before seeing the doctor. After the onceover by that doctor a short while later, Jezz was now furiously trying to remember everything he could about what had happened since speaking to Keith over the computer.

Teemu looked around the room for something to write on, before grabbing the chart from the bottom of the bed. "What about this? There's a pen attached."

Jezz held his hand out, gesturing impatiently for it, then grabbed the chart. He turned the paper over on the clipboard. The other side was blank and, even better, there were two sheets, both blank on the reverse. Jezz didn't stop to look at the front, just started scribbling furiously.

Teemu watched him, his face a slow-motion riot of glacial confusion.

"You okay, man?"

"I'm fine. Got any cigarettes?" Jezz didn't look up.

Teemu patted his pockets, futilely. "I'm all out."

Still Jezz didn't look up from the paper. "Then how about you go get me some."

Teemu, scratching at his beard, agreed and left.

Jezz sat in the wheelchair, the charts he'd scribbled on wadded up tightly in his fist as Price wheeled him down the corridor. The hospital had discharged him on the grounds that there was little they could do for him now. There were plenty of far more urgent cases they needed to deal with. Price and Teemu were taking him back to their temporary billet. Price had secured the crew a seventy-two-hour leave, in the hope that after that time, Jezz would be fit enough to return to duty. It was that, or shipping Jezz home and taking on two new crew, which Price was reluctant to do after their experience with Nora 2.

Jezz was set on not going home. Something was telling him that he needed to be here, in the thick of the action, at least until he'd sorted the psychosis out. If there was any chance of doing that here and so not returning home a burned-out nutjob, he had to take it.

Outside the front of the hospital, Jezz shivered slightly in his uniform. The sky was clear and the sun felt good on his skin, but while the unnatural cold of the Eltiy'ch was dissipating, it was still far from normal weather for the time of year. They waited a few minutes for their jeep to arrive, then Teemu helped get Jezz into the front before climbing in the back with Price.

"Hey! Take it easy!" Price yelled at the driver as the jeep lurched away from the pavement. "Our guy's wounded here!"

The driver saluted, without turning round, and completely ignored him, weaving the jeep in and out of traffic on the way back to the hotel.

At the other end, Teemu and Price again helped Jezz out of the jeep, Price scowling at the driver as they did so. They offered to take him up to the room, but Jezz declined. "Have they got a bar here?"

"Yeah, it's pretty miserable, but sure."

The three of them went into the bar and found a table easily. The bar was frequented by a number of the older officers billeted in the hotel, much to the dismay of the hotel owner, as he watched their presence drive most of the rank-and-file soldiers out to the local bars. With the billeting imposed on him, the bar was his only way of making any money at all from the war, and the few customers he was getting were hardly making him rich, despite the stupid prices he was able to charge.

The campaign seemed to be turning a corner. The pushback against the Eltiy'ch had been more successful than anyone expected. This was met with a certain amount of scepticism by command, as their own capability and tactics hadn't changed significantly, they were just successfully pushing the Eltiy'ch back. Ziyang was virtually free again now and with increased British air support expected within twelve hours, they were making plans to clear the whole of Sichuan province of the invading aliens. What had changed for the Eltiy'ch, no one knew. Supply issues, internal politics, a lack of stomach for the extended campaign they'd been forced into… A number of theories were doing the rounds amongst the troops. "For all we know," said Price, "they came here for something specific that they now have and don't need Earth anymore." There were those higher up, however, who feared a trap, feared being drawn into an advance they couldn't sustain and getting crushed in a flanking manoeuvre. But as the alternative to taking the bait was just sitting where they were and giving their adversary a chance to regroup, they felt there was little choice but to push the advantage and hope the incoming air support would swing it.

Price outlined all this to Jezz while the three of them sipped at their local beers. "So, we're heading back to Chongqing?"

"Could be," replied Price. "Although we've been attached to a new division, so it depends on their orders. Could be Chongqing, or north-east up into Hubei province, maybe even Guizhou. We roll out in three days, so we find out then, I guess." The atmosphere in the hotel bar was sapping what little good spirit he had. "You going to be any good by then?"

Jezz rolled his neck and shoulders, wincing as he did so. "I think so. I guess. I mean, at least I'm not marching anywhere, right? I might not be able to get in and out of the tank so quickly, but I can do my job."

Teemu looked glum. "It's not a good idea, Price. If he can't get out… I mean, we're winning now, aren't we? There can't be the same need for every possible fighting man and woman. Maybe he should go home, see his family."

"Well, it's up to him." Price took a moody swig of his beer, then wiped his sleeve across his moustache.

"Look, if I get a good night's sleep tonight, take it easy tomorrow and then again tomorrow night, we can decide then. I don't want to leave you guys with two new crew, that's not good either. The ReadiSet is doing its business, it's just muscle fatigue now. Another thirty-six hours, I could feel like new. Besides…"

He paused, causing the other two men to look at him intently. Jezz leaned into the table.

"Look, I think what's going on my head is related to all this," he waved his hand vaguely around them.

"Well, yeah, fallout from the phero-grenade," said Price, frowning. "But that's wearing off, right?"

"It is and it isn't. I don't know. But no, I think it's more than that. I think whatever's going on is coming from something deeper inside. Maybe triggered by the phero-grenade, sure, but responding to something in me. The things I see, the place I go to…" Jezz leaned back again in his chair, stubbing out his cigarette. "I don't know, I just feel like I need to be here, in China I mean, to deal with this. I'm not ready to go home a burned-out vet." Jezz polished off his beer and waved the empty bottle at the barman. "While I've got fight left in me, I want to fight."

Jezz had declined a third drink, instead letting Teemu help him upstairs to their room. It was only mid-afternoon, but Jezz was serious about resting up as much as possible to ensure he was combat-ready. This latest episode had left him with a renewed focus, a determination to finish this once and for all.

"Suite 86, home from home."

Jezz ignored the flourish with which Teemu gestured at the pit they'd been allocated. The army had rammed as many cots as possible into each room, in an attempt to house as many men as they could. Their room was just big enough to house the regular bed and three fold-downs, and still give the men room to walk around. The room had its own bathroom, but sharing with Teemu, Jezz wasn't sure that was a plus point. He lay down on the bed that the other two insisted he take. "Who's in the other one?"

"Nora 3."

"They've been assigned?"

"Not yet, but we're expecting them this evening. Get some rest."

"Sure. Look Teemu, do me a favour. If you're heading out to get drunk, try and keep it down when you come in, yeah?"

"What do you mean 'if'?"

"I'm serious."

"Ya, ya, I promise." The big man waved as he shut the door behind him. In a few minutes, Jezz was fast asleep.

He awoke to find the room in semi-darkness. It was night, but the blinds were still up, so light from the city cast its shadows over the walls. Jezz laid there for a few minutes, his head facing the window, before realising he wasn't alone.

On the cot at the foot of his bed, a slim figure was perched, their face illuminated by the glow of their phone.

"Hey."

The face looked up, and Jezz saw it was a young woman. Thin, with straggly red hair and prominent freckles, a thin mouth and heavy-lidded eyes. "Hey," she replied in a husky voice.

"You're Nora 3?"

"Excuse me?"

"Sorry, I mean, you're our new loader/operator?"

"I guess so. Quinn."

"Hi Quinn. Jezz."

"Yeah, the big guy told me. Well, slurred something that sounded like that. To be honest I thought he said your name was Jeff, but okay. Hi Jezz."

Jezz stiffened slightly. It was, of course, perfectly easy to believe Teemu's drunken pronunciation could have come out like that, and it wasn't like Jeff was a made-up word. But the name sent a shiver of disquiet down Jezz's back.

"You got a signal?" He asked, pointing at the woman's phone, as much to change the subject as out of any interest.

"What, this? Nah, just got a few books still on it. I haven't been able to use it properly for weeks, but I can still see the shit on it I downloaded."

Jezz nodded, slowly, and reached for his cigarettes. He winced as he rolled over, and again as he rolled back.

"I'm sorry, man, you want some help with that? You don't look great."

Jezz waved his hand dismissively. "I'm fine, need to start moving a bit anyway."

"You okay? I didn't realise you were injured."

"It's nothing, fell awkwardly. Just need to rest a bit."

"Drunk, eh? Not surprised, the company you keep."

"Something like that. Look, Teemu's okay, guy's just got an appetite." Jezz lit a cigarette, then remembered himself. "Sorry, you don't mind?"

"Nah, it's cool. You got one?"

Jezz tossed her a cigarette and his lighter, watching her face light up in the flare of the lighter's flame.

"So how come you got saddled with us?"

"Last crew all bought it, barely got out myself." Quinn held up her right arm which, in the dim light coming in from the city outside, Jezz could see was still bandaged extensively.

"I'm sorry."

Quinn shrugged. "War."

"Right."

There was quiet for a few minutes as they smoked. Jezz found himself ruminating on his psychoses again. He surreptitiously felt under his pillow to check that his notes were still there. It all seemed so real while he was in it. Jeff's memories, his *life*, all of that was so imbedded, and it was getting harder to shake the personality off when he came back around. It was so immersive. Jezz thought about 'his' sister Anoushka, how that relationship seemed so defined, had real history. Of course, the fact the psychoses ran deep didn't prove anything. The chemical weapons of the Eltiy'ch were completely outside of human experience, who knew what reactions they could induce in the human brain? It was terrifying, yet perfectly feasible to conceive of a deluded state that extended so deeply and thoroughly. And yet Jezz could still, if he concentrated hard enough…

"What about your loader?"

The question shook him out of his reverie, confusing him for a moment. "Oh, she went home, had enough. Wanted to be with her family when it looked like… you know."

"She? I was told I was replacing a man."

Jezz took a moment. "Oh, right, Nora 2." He felt bad at having forgotten the young Swiss; the boy's face with its single, fatal bullet wound, loomed in his vision. "He was shot."

"Nora 2?"

"He wasn't around for long enough to get to know him. We called him that because, well, he replaced Nora 1. Nora, our Nora."

Our Nora. That mention of her took Jezz back to that night by the river, when they'd fucked in the alleyway. He shook his head to clear the recollection from his mind. "Anyway, she left, he came, and two hours later we landed in a tank trap on the push to the Tuo, had to evacuate. In the firefight, he got shot."

"Tough break."

"Really was. He joined us in the morning and was dead by the afternoon. Couldn't tell you his name with a gun to my head."

"Encouraging."

Jezz gave a humourless laugh. "It was a shitty break. It happens."

"War," Quinn shrugged again.

"Uhuh."

Quinn got up and went into the bathroom. She didn't turn the light on, so the fan didn't come on to mask the sound of her pissing. A year ago, this would have freaked Jezz out, but the imminent death of mankind had a way of breaking down social convention. Now he thought nothing of it.

Except, a year ago. The thought awakened something in the back of his mind. He could remember a year ago, when he, Price and Nora had landed, bought their shares in the tank that seemed like a better bet than signing up to infantry. He could remember meeting Teemu, the qualified driver they needed to complete their crew. It was all as clear as day, no memory loss or blank, no reason to fear it wasn't lived experience. But then, as Jeff, he'd felt the same when he woke up in the Ziyang hospital, no sense that *his* memories and emotions weren't real. For the first time, a horrifying question formulated in Jezz's mind – was he absolutely sure that *this* was reality, that *he* wasn't the psychosis?

His whole body spasmed with nausea at the thought, threatening to overwhelm him.

"Whoa, whoa, whoa," said Quinn, coming out of the bathroom and running over to him as she saw his body writhing. She put a hand on his arm to try and calm him.

"Bin… sick…"

She looked around and grabbed the wastepaper basket by the bed, bringing it round to the side Jezz was leaning over. She held it as he emptied the contents of his stomach into it. He was glad there wasn't much in there to expel, as, no doubt, was she. After three or four retches, he flaked onto his back and lay there, panting.

"You okay there, sport?"

Jezz could barely summon the energy to acknowledge the question with a wave. As his hand flopped over again, it fell on his cigarettes. He instinctively drew one out.

"I'm not so sure that's a good… Oh, okay, you're doing it… Cool…"

Jezz drew on the cigarette, then exhaled a plume of smoke straight up. "Get rid… the taste."

"No, fair enough. You want some water? I'm just going to go get rid of this."

Quinn took the bin into the bathroom and Jezz could hear her pour his watery vomit out into the toilet, before giving the bin a hasty rinse out in the bath. She reappeared with a glass of water which he took, gratefully. Sipping at it tentatively a couple of times, he then let Quinn take it back off him and stand it down on the floor beside his bed.

She took a seat on the bed next to him, cocking her head as she looked at him quizzically.

"What gives?"

"I dunno, reaction to the painkillers? Shock? Who knows."

But it wasn't that, and even as he fought to stop his mind returning to that awful question, it continued to burn brightly enough at the back of his mind that he couldn't shake it.

Who's the psychosis here? Jeff? Or me?

By the time Price and Teemu rolled in just before midnight, Quinn and Jezz were sat up next to each other in his bed. Or rather, he was in it, she was sat on the covers. Jezz was pleasantly surprised to see that Teemu, while most definitely drunk, wasn't utterly wasted. He might even, had Jezz been asleep, have been able to get in without waking him. Price seemed in good spirits, which only happened when he drank, but likewise wasn't noticeably ruined.

"You're still up? I thought you needed rest."

"That's probably my fault," said Quinn.

"And you are?"

"This is Nora 3," said Jezz, a wry grin on his face. Quinn elbowed him in the ribs, causing him to wince with the pain.

Teemu muttered something as he flopped down onto the cot nearest the door, which Jezz assumed was a remark along the lines that he'd told Price that earlier and why didn't anyone ever listen to him. But Price didn't respond and Teemu didn't seem to notice. Instead, the Finn pulled his boots off, toppled to one side like a fallen tree, and was asleep in seconds, grunting to himself.

Quinn scooted off the bed and offered a hand to Price, who shook it. "Quinn."

"Price. I'm the commander. You've met Jezz, gunner. That's Teemu, driver."

"Yes indeed."

Price looked her in the eye for a few moments, before seeming to reach a decision in his own mind. He gave her a short nod. "Okay. Let's get some sleep. This idiot needs the rest, and you could do with getting to sleep before that travesty starts snoring."

"That's not him snoring?"

"Oh, believe me, he's just tuning up the band."

Jezz grinned as he pulled the sheet up and carefully rolled onto his side.

By the morning, the room was thick with an unhealthy atmosphere of bodies and stale farts. Jezz was glad he'd been sick the night before, or he might be awfully tempted to have a go now. He sat up in bed, surprised to see daylight slicing in through the gap in the curtains. Clearly it was quite late.

Except for Teemu's still unconscious form, he was alone, no sign of Price or Quinn. Price wasn't a surprise, he rarely slept in. After a relatively early night like the one before, he'd probably been up for hours. As for Quinn, presumably she'd woken up, taken one whiff of the odour in here and legged it. Jezz lit a cigarette, partly to try and kill his sense of smell.

He realised, to his great relief, that he wasn't aching nearly as much as he had been the day before. Between the fall in the computer room and the hand-to-hand with the Eltiy'ch, he'd been fearing he'd be laid up for days. Though he didn't feel great, the improvement was encouraging. He got out of bed and dressed, slowly. He started to tiptoe out of the room, but Teemu broke into another bout of snoring and Jezz realised it wasn't necessary to be making any effort not to wake him. The bear would likely sleep until sundown. Jezz slammed the door on the way out.

He had no plans to go far, but equally figured it wouldn't do him good to lay in bed all day. Taking it easy was all well and good, but the last thing he needed was to stiffen up. He needed to move around for a bit, limber up. An enquiry with a sergeant in the front lobby revealed that he wouldn't find any food in the hotel, but there was a place down the block that would still be serving and, what's more, they served Western food.

Sold on that, thought Jezz. Noodles were great, but they'd been in China a long time now, and eaten almost nothing for months but basic rations and local cuisine. Even the thought of breakfast pancakes almost had him breaking out into a run. Or it would have done, had that been remotely possible.

He found the place easily enough. It was no surprise to find it full of Western troops jumping at the chance for some familiar fare. He almost despaired of getting a seat when he saw Quinn waving to him from a table near the back. Giving her a thumbs up, he was about to join the queue at the counter when she beckoned him over.

"Don't be stupid, take a seat, I'll go get you something. What do you want?"

Jezz accepted the offer with relief, easing himself into the seat opposite. "Coffee. And they do pancakes?"

Quinn nodded and left him at the table. He took his

cigarettes out, dropped them on the table and lit one. A soldier on the next table gave him an annoyed look, but Jezz gave him the finger and the man turned back to his friends.

It was a big place, laid out like a canteen, and was doing a roaring trade. Given the situation with the bar, this place was probably why their hotel wasn't even bothering to cater for breakfasts. Jezz looked around, nodded at a few faces he recognised and waited for Quinn to come back. When she did, she came bearing pancakes, butter and a jug of maple syrup, along with two cups of strong black coffee.

"Not both for you, soldier," she said as she put it down in front of her seat.

Jezz grinned at her, which she didn't return.

Looking at her for the first time in daylight, Jezz could see an ugly scar that ran from her right ear down her jawline. There were signs of burns on her neck on that side too.

"Pretty grim, huh."

He hadn't realised he was staring. "I'm sorry."

Quinn dismissed his apology with a wave. "We're all carrying shit. You don't look so great yourself."

He frowned, something about her words striking a chord, a memory. Then it was gone.

"That's the truth."

She had a tomboyish look, and Jezz already had the impression she didn't smile much naturally. But she'd been friendly enough the night before, and as they drank their coffee and Jezz polished off his pancakes, they talked; about the action they'd seen, and about home. Quinn gave him a reappraising look when he told her the story of his wrestling with the Eltiy'ch, then recoiled slightly as he told her about Price shooting the bound creature out of hand.

"Was that really necessary?"

Jezz shrugged. "He's never said anything, but he took Nora 2 dying pretty badly." He stabbed at another forkful of pancake. "And he was right, this wasn't like picking up a foreign soldier, where you can maybe get hold of a translator. This is an alien life form from another planet. Hell, we wouldn't even know how to feed it in captivity. And who knows what it might be capable of when it healed, or what diseases they might carry. I was an idiot to even try to capture it. I should have shot it the first chance I got."

"You showed a basic human tendency toward compassion, I don't think you should kick yourself too hard for that."

"You said it, a basic *human* tendency. I doubt that thing would have thought twice about finishing me off."

"True," conceded Quinn, but she looked uncomfortable. "You seen Price this morning? He was gone when I woke up."

"He doesn't sleep late. He barely sleeps at all, truth be told. We're halfway through a seventy-two-hour leave, he could have gone anywhere. Maybe even tried to get a lift out of town, find a bar somewhere quiet. He'll be back before he needs to be, though, ready to shepherd us back to the tank. And get Teemu out of whatever bullshit mess he finds himself in."

"Yeah, he seems quite the character." Quinn's tone was decidedly arch.

Jezz grinned to himself as he looked down at his plate, guiding the last few bits of pancake onto his fork. "He is that. Helluva tankman, though. Don't judge him on last night. When he needs to be, he's there."

"Sure. You guys seem tight, and Price doesn't seem like the sort to carry anyone."

"You're not wrong there." Jezz mopped up the remains of his maple syrup, then drained his coffee. "Fancy a walk?"

Quinn nodded and they left.

He'd never intended to tell her. Letting her go into combat knowing their gunner was nuts seemed a little unsettling. But then again, in the end Jezz figured that letting her go into combat not knowing their gunner was nuts wasn't exactly fair either. It was pretty much a no-win situation, so in the end he just came out with it.

She wasn't the warmest person he'd ever met, but something about her placid, objective demeanour made her easier to talk to than Price or Teemu. They sat on a bench in a playground across from a burnt-out office block, passing a bottle of whisky back and forth as Jezz told Quinn all he could remember about the phero-attack, and everything that had spun out from it. The patchy recollections of this other, past life he'd experienced, the sense of disconnect from this world, the pale woman, all of it. She listened patiently, interrupting only every now and then with a question. He referred to his notes, which he'd secured in his combat trousers, and when he was done, the sense of relief was immense, draining almost. Part of him wanted to go to sleep on the bench right there and then.

He looked at her. "I guess getting in a tank with me seems like a pretty stupid idea right now, huh."

She shrugged. "You're no crazier than my last gunner, that guy was out of his mind. And that was recreational drugs, couldn't even blame the bugs for that."

"The worrying thing is not knowing when it's going to happen."

"Not strictly true. You said every time it's happened, you've seen the pale woman beforehand. So you know exactly when it's going to happen. Have you seen her since you woke up the last time?"

"No," Jezz admitted.

"There you go. Until you do, it's all good. And when you do, we can prepare for it."

"And if it happens in the midst of a firefight?"

"Then it does. Won't affect us any worse than if you got shot. And that could happen to any of us at any time. Seems to me like you're no more of a liability than anyone who can go down in combat. And believe me, there's plenty of guys out there who in any normal warzone would have been shipped home months ago. This is all hands to the pump; this is our world we're fighting for here. Not oil, not water, not some New York billionaire crook's re-election campaign. Humanity itself." Jezz looked at her, the grim look of determination on her face as she looked out over the ruined street. "We don't push every last one of these fuckers into the sea, it's game over." Any squeamishness over Price's shooting of the prisoner forgotten, she clearly meant business.

"I guess you're right."

"Damned straight, I'm right." Quinn dropped her cigarette butt on the floor and ground it into the dirt with her boot.

"It's just…" Jezz struggled to even say it.

"What?"

"This sounds so stupid. Crazier than any of it."

"Spit it out, soldier."

"When I puked last night, in the hotel room?"

"Yeah?"

"I got nauseous because a thought too fucking weird to process had just jumped into my head." Jezz took another swig of whisky. "Oh boy. Okay, so what if… What if that other life I'm hallucinating… isn't."

"Isn't what?"

"A hallucination."

"What?"

"When I'm the other guy, Jeff, his whole life seems… unquestionable. He doesn't just know people, he remembers them, remembers growing up with them. What if that's because he's real? I keep asking myself, is he my psychosis? Or am I his?"

Quinn stared at him, then grabbed the whisky from him, knocked it back. "Holy shit, you really are crazy. You think I'm a hallucination?"

"I'm not saying that's what I think. I'm saying, what if? You know? I mean, I'm sure if Jeff had this conversation with Anoush, she'd be as indignant as you are right now. How do I know what's real?"

"You think you're not real."

"No! That's exactly the point. I don't think that at all. I'm convinced I'm real. I have memories, family, all that. I am one hundred per cent convinced I'm real. But so's he." Jeff shrugged, unable to make eye contact. "And we can't both be right."

Quinn, still looking at him, didn't say anything for a minute, then shook her head and took another slug of whisky.

"Well, shit."

Jezz didn't sleep that night, just lay awake listening to Teemu's snoring. Price hadn't returned and Quinn had been weird with him ever since their walk, hanging onto and drinking the rest of the whisky. She passed out soon after they got back to their billet. Not that he could blame her. Having someone tell you they thought you might not exist was pretty crazy; when that person was someone your life might depend upon tomorrow, it was downright scary. Was that the only possibility? Did it have to be him or Jeff? Could it be both, somehow? Some sort of... telepathy? Jezz shook his head. As if this was helping. Hell, why stop there? If it could be both, couldn't it also be neither? Maybe everything he perceived, both here and there, was just some kind of fantasy. Hell, maybe he was a character in some kind of alien entertainment, brought to life to... *I mean, honestly, what the fuck? I think, therefore I am, isn't that, like, philosophy 101? If*

So Jezz lay there, questions swirling in his brain. It was not quite so cold in Ziyang now, and they'd decided to open the window to try and clear some of the disgusting fug. If anything suggested the Eltiy'ch retreat was genuine, it was the warmer weather. Although, as Price pointed out, they couldn't ignore the possibility that, given their ability to manipulate the weather, this was also part of their ruse to lure the human forces into a trap. Trust Price to suggest that. Jezz, though, had reached the point where he didn't care. Command had the right idea, as far as he was concerned. If the Eltiy'ch were retreating, they had to press. This wasn't a war, this was a fight to the death. Letting them fall back and regroup wasn't an option now. Quinn had it figured best. They had to do everything they could to push the fuckers into the sea. Now all Jezz wanted to do was get this last day of waiting over and get back in the fight.

He toyed with the idea of going for a walk but was wary of ending up somewhere he shouldn't. And besides, as much as he couldn't sleep, physically he was tired, his body aching now he was laying down, processing the movement of the day.

Eventually he did get up, but instead of heading down to the street, he took the stairs up until he came out onto the roof. Going over to the edge, he lit a cigarette and stared out over the foreign city, the red glow of fire ever-present but now even further away, way out beyond the Tuo. He couldn't even hear gunfire from here, and realised he couldn't remember the last time he could have said that. There was still plenty of noise, of course. Drunken soldiers, waiting for their turn to roll out, cruised the streets. From somewhere below, Jezz could hear the telltale sounds of a brawl, shouts of encouragement turning to calls to flee as the MPs appeared. Civilians were also starting to drift back into the city, looking to make a quick profit from the armies and militias; selling their booze, their food and their flesh. Somewhere off to the north, someone was letting off fireworks, colourful blooms erupting periodically and showering down into nothingness. Probably some local family celebrating being able to return to their home. Jezz watched, transfixed. He felt as if he could almost taste the acrid taste of gunpowder in the back of his throat...

"Pretty, isn't it."

Jezz spun around. By the door to the stairwell stood the pale woman, wearing some kind of hooded garment that left her face in shadow, leaning against the wall. He went to take a step back but stopped himself. If he was about to pass out, best not to be standing by the edge of the roof. Instead, he stepped towards her.

"What do you want?"

"I want us to take responsibility."

"What does that even mean? Us? Responsibility for what? What are you talking about?"

"This drifting between two worlds, running away every time things get too stressful. It's no good." The woman coughed, hacking up phlegm that she spat, unceremoniously, onto the ground.

"What do you mean, running away? I came over here voluntarily, I stood up for this." Jezz flung an arm out and gestured at the warzone surrounding them.

"I'm not talking about the war, Jezz. We need to wake up, dammit. Work out what's happening to us, how we stop it."

"Why do you keep talking about us? You're the cause of this; I flip out every time *you* appear! Maybe if you left me alone, maybe that's how it would stop. You think of that?"

The woman didn't respond. Instead, she pushed herself away from the wall and turned around, stepped into the stairwell and left.

Jezz remained stood on the roof, shivering in a way that had nothing to do with the temperature.

When he awoke the next morning, Teemu and Quinn were still passed out drunk in their cots. Price, standing by the window, gave him a grunt of acknowledgement.

"You're back, then," said Jezz.

"How are you feeling?"

"I ache, but I'm okay."

"Breakfast?"

The two men left the hotel and headed down to the canteen. It was still early. The place was barely half-full, chatter was minimal. Jezz chose a table for them while Price went up to the counter. When he came over to the table bearing a tray, Jezz gasped.

"Is that actual bacon?"

"Yep. With the new air support, they're shoring up the supply chains again. Seems like we're really turning this around."

Jezz stubbed out his cigarette and grabbed the jar of maple syrup, pouring a generous helping over his pancakes and bacon. "Holy hell, that smells amazing."

Price gave him a rare grin. "You're not wrong. Decent coffee for once, as well."

They set upon their meal with vigour, polishing off the food with almost indecent haste. After the last crumbs were gone, they leaned back, sighing with satisfaction.

"I haven't felt this good in months," Price remarked.

Jezz looked at him, trying to mask his surprise. Price, far from chatty at the best of times, never really let on anything about how he was feeling. Yet Jezz had to admit, Price did indeed look better than he had in months. Moustache trimmed, eyes less bloodshot. Three parts sober, if Jezz was any judge. He'd even combed his hair. Maybe the leave and the developments in the war were breaking through the wall Price had been building around himself since their first taste of combat. Jezz thought it best not to comment on it. "It certainly makes a change to get some decent food."

Price didn't make eye contact as he asked, "So how are you doing, Jezz? Really?"

Ah. So that was it. Breakfast and some chat, to preface the Talk.

"I'm okay. Like I said, aching like hell, but so much better than when I woke up in the hospital. And I've been working on getting movement back in my arm, limbering up." By way of a demonstration, Jezz rotated his shoulder a couple of times, managing to stifle a wince.

"And the crazy?"

Jezz toyed with a cigarette, not lighting it. He stared at it intently, uncertain of what to say.

"Jezz, come on, I've known you since High School, and I'm not blind. This war brought you alive, gave you purpose, but since the phero-blast... It's not just the blackouts, it's your whole attitude. It's like you're not really here..."

"I saw her again last night," said Jezz interrupting. "The pale woman I see before the episodes. Spoke to her, up on the roof."

"Okay. And, what? This means you're about to..." Price trailed off, making a circular motion with the hand he was holding his cigarette in.

"I don't know. I mean, yes, that's the pattern. But she left. I didn't run from her, she left. And... Well, I feel okay. Haven't seen her this morning."

Price took another mouthful of coffee, then a long drag on his cigarette.

"We don't roll out until tomorrow. I guess by then either you'll have gone, or you won't."

Jezz looked down into his mug. "I guess so."

They were silent for a while, the low early morning

chatter of soldiers around them the backdrop to their awkward pause. It was Price who spoke first.

"I think you need to go home."

Jezz looked up. "What?"

Price ran a hand through his hair, then looked Jezz straight in the eye. "I think you need to go home, Jezz. Look, we grew up together, I know your parents. I don't want to have to be the one to tell them you died out here because you kept on fighting when you were sick. Nor do I want to die in my tank because my gunner's passed out in his seat in the thick of battle. You're fucked up, this war has fucked you up, and I don't know how to help you. I want to help you, Jezz, but I don't know how, and I don't know that I can. So go home."

"I… I can't. I can't leave you and Teemu here, that's not right."

"Nora went. You didn't seem to object to that."

"Of course not," Jezz, trying to formulate his words, held out his hands as if a coherent argument could be summoned from the air, "it's… Look, Nora left. I wholeheartedly agreed with her right to do so. And I'd feel exactly the same if you or Teemu wanted to go. We're all volunteers here, we signed up voluntarily, our contracts give us the right to leave if we want to. I wouldn't blame anyone for wanting to see their family again. We all get to make our own choices, Price. But just because I don't have the right to judge anyone else, doesn't mean I won't judge myself." He picked up Price's lighter and angrily sparked it into life, holding it to the tip of his cigarette. He dropped the lighter, pushing it back to Price. "*I* need to stay. *I* couldn't forgive myself if I left. I can't hold anyone to account except myself. So no, I didn't judge Nora, but it wouldn't be right for me."

"And if you black out during combat? If Teemu or I get shot because we can't get out of our disabled tank quick enough because we're carrying you?"

Jezz slumped in his seat, rubbing his face. "I don't know, I don't know. I hear you, Matt. I get what you're saying completely, but I can't go home. Not yet." He looked up at Price. "I think whatever's happening to me, I need to find a way to stop it, and I just feel like I'm only going to find that here. I don't think running away…"

At the words 'running away', the words of the pale woman came back to him. Price frowned as he watched the colour drain from Jezz's face.

"What is it?"

"She said that, those exact words. She said that running away was no good. I had to wake up, work out what was happening."

"Who? Who said that? Quinn?"

"No, the woman. The…" Again, Jezz gestured in place of words that wouldn't form. "On the roof, last night."

"Wait, you mean you *actually* talked to her? Had a conversation?"

Jezz nodded.

"This hallucination, she spoke to you and told you not to run away. And that's why you won't leave." Price's face was a mask of disbelief.

"I know it sounds crazy…"

"You're fucking right it sounds fucking crazy." Price stood up and dropped his cigarette butt in the dregs of his coffee. His moustache quivered as he scowled at Jezz. "I tried, Jezz. But you really are off-the-fucking-chart-losing-it. If I thought I could replace you without Teemu pitching a fit, I'd do it in a heartbeat. But whatever, I can't deal with this."

And with that, he left.

Jezz didn't try to follow him. Instead, after giving Price time to disappear, he stood up and made his own way from the canteen. Out on the street, he paused for a moment, wondering which way to go. He had no agenda, nothing to do, and there was still twenty-four hours before he had to check in for the rollout.

He set off, choosing a direction at random, wandering through the city with no goal or aim. It was remarkable how quickly life was returning to the streets. Refugees who had had nowhere to go and no way to get there were now streaming back into the city to find out what was left of their homes. Jezz bought a bottle of some unfamiliar Chinese soft drink at a market that had opened up. He watched families entering buildings, some still intact, some little more than empty shells. Here and there, groups of people picked through the rubble of a ruined building, looking for lost family heirlooms or just salvaging whatever they could find. Soldiers, some in packs, some in ones and twos, wandered the streets looking for bars or women. On street corners and looking down from windows, local women, dressed provocatively, called out to the passing soldiers, trying to entice them to part with their cash in return for some company. Few of them called out to Jezz. He was clearly giving off some kind of aura, for which he was grateful.

He found himself near the Tuo and made a decisive move in the direction of the river. Emerging onto the quay, he realised he was not far from where he and Nora… well, from there. He bought a pancake from an old woman who looked vaguely familiar and stood on the quay, watching the boats as he ate his snack. Here, too, there were signs of a return to normality. People on boats shouted to friends and acquaintances on the quay, and there were occasional outbursts of cheering as every now and then a boat, piled high with food, moored up and started to unload. Jezz could hardly credit the change in atmosphere since the last time he stood here, just a matter of days ago, when it felt like Ziyang was hours from falling.

A small cargo boat chugged past, a dirty great diesel engine pumping out thick, acrid smoke. Jezz coughed in the craft's wake as the smoke stung his throat.

Price's words echoed in his mind. Jezz didn't need to ask himself if the other man was right. He knew he was a liability, that he could black out at any time. If that happened in combat, he would be jeopardising the lives of his friends. But that didn't mean that Jezz could go home. He knew he had to stay, had to stand by his friends. The paradox was tearing him up. To stand by his friends meant to endanger them, but he couldn't leave them here. And he'd spoken the truth to Price. He didn't blame Nora for leaving, any more than he would blame Teemu or Price for leaving. Hell, if they both decided to go home, he'd gladly join them, there was no need for him to stay here without them. Or was there? That feeling in his gut that the psychoses he was experiencing could only be stopped by seeing this out wouldn't go away, despite there being no feasible explanation for it. And as Quinn had said, any one of them could be incapacitated during combat, for any number of reasons.

"Shit," he muttered to himself. This was intolerable.

"So, take action."

Jezz didn't even turn around. "What?"

"You feel paralysed by indecision. If this is so intolerable, make a choice, *make* something happen. Break this cycle we're in and *move us forward*."

Jezz pulled out a cigarette and lit it, stalling for time as his mind tried to piece itself together.

"I need to go back first." He turned around to face the pale woman, who stood close behind him, her hood pulled forward, shading her face. She lifted one slender, impossibly pale-skinned arm.

"Oh fuck..." Jezz stayed conscious just long enough to hear his nose crack.

10

Jezz opened his eyes. A ceiling, not the sky. For a moment, there was the dizzying sensation that the ceiling was just inches from his face, but his eyes were deceiving him. He blinked twice, three times, and the ceiling retreated to a more realistic distance. "Okay, where are we...?" He fought to get his breathing under control, to calm his mind and process what he was seeing. While he lay there, he raised a hand to his face and tentatively touched his nose. He yelped, then coughed. Blood mixed with phlegm as he wiped his hand on his shirt. "Oh, for crying out loud..."

His yelping appeared to attract attention and he heard footsteps outside the room, then the door opened. Exhausted and battered as he felt, he didn't look over, just stayed staring at the ceiling.

"Jeff?"

"Quinn?"

"What? Who's Quinn?"

Jezz blinked rapidly, shaking his head as much as he dared to try and clear his thoughts. The footsteps came closer and a face appeared at the corner of his vision. A blonde face. Familiar, yet strange. Flushed, he noted.

"Jeff, it's me, Sal. Are you okay?"

Jezz looked at the woman and frowned. "Sal...?"

The woman bent over him. She held the back of her hand to his forehead, before stroking his head. Jezz was taken aback to realise his scalp was shaved. "Shhh, try to get some rest, baby. You were hit by a cyclist."

The cyclist, the bookshop, wait… "Oh God…"

Jeff experienced an overwhelming wave of nausea and rolled over. There was a bowl beside the bed, as if this had been foreseen. He threw up. After a minute, panting, he threw up again. The way the thick, honey-like vomit seemed to cling to his throat, coating the inside of his mouth made him retch. He wiped his mouth and rolled onto his back. "Sal, Sal, where am I?"

"You're at home, honey, at Anya's." Sal sat on the bed next to him and took his hand. "You went into town and got hit by a cyclist. Nothing too serious, just bruises mainly. I'm afraid you did make a bit of a mess of your nose when you fell."

"My nose…" Something about the reference to his nose jolted his brain. "Sal, can you get me my notebook."

"Your notebook?"

"Yeah, it was in my bag. I had a bag with me, my bag, it was in my bag…"

"Okay, okay, calm down. I'll go ask Anya."

Sal, concern written all over her face, got up and left the room.

Jeff lay as still as he could, focusing all his concentration on trying to remember everything he could until Sal came back. "Is this it?"

Jeff reached out and took it. "Yeah, that's the one. Pen?"

"Of, of course." She disappeared again.

"Come on, come on…" he muttered to himself. He had to get as much down as possible before it slipped away. He snatched the pen from her when she returned, then waved at her frantically to leave. She couldn't hide the hurt on her face as she did so, but if Jeff noticed it, he didn't react. He just started scribbling furiously.

Jeff made his way, slowly, downstairs. He found Sal in the kitchen with Anoush. His half-sister fixed him with an icy stare, and he noticed Sal's eyes were red. He went over to her and wrapped his arms around her. "I'm sorry," he whispered. "I just needed to get everything down before I forgot it. It doesn't stay in my brain for long and I need to understand what's happening to me." He gently rested his forehead against hers and closed his eyes. "I'm glad you're here, truly." He kissed her, then kissed her again, on the forehead. Sal brushed a tear away, nodding at him to show she understood.

He stepped back, swaying a little.

"Are you sure you ought to be up?" asked Anoush, defrosting a little.

"I don't know. I am, so I guess so. There's a smell of vomit in my room, anyway." He idly petted Giora as Anoush rolled her eyes at him.

"I'll go clear that up then, shall I?"

"I can do it," said Sal.

"No, it's fine." Anoush left the room.

"I could have gone."

"It's fine, don't worry about it, she loves playing the martyr. It all went in the bowl anyway. All she has to do is empty it. Where's Anya?"

"Outside. Do you want a drink?"

"I could murder a tea."

"Are you sure? You've just been sick. Would a cold drink be better?"

Jeff looked at her quizzically.

"I don't know, less rich?"

"Fine, just water then. I'll be outside." He kissed her forehead again.

Jeff let himself carefully down into the low Adirondack chair next to Anya's. "Hey."

She held out a hand to him and, when he was sat, he reached out and gave it a squeeze. "You're back with us, darling."

"Seems like."

"How are you feeling?"

"Like I was hit by a cyclist."

Anya laughed and offered him a cigarette. He looked at it for a moment before declining.

"Just been sick."

"Ah. Not all over my carpet again, I hope."

"No, I made the bowl this time."

"Good boy. And besides that?"

"Sore, stiff, but I'm okay. How come I'm here, didn't anyone call an ambulance?"

"Of course, but they checked you out, they seemed happy you didn't have a concussion or anything. No permanent damage, so they let you come home."

"While I was still out of it?"

Anya looked at him, visibly puzzled. "You weren't unconscious, darling. You weren't talking much but you were awake. You don't remember?"

"I was awake?"

"Of course. Like I said, you didn't say much, but you were conscious when we left the hospital."

Jeff stared at her. "But I... I had an episode."

Anya nodded. "I figured. You didn't seem yourself, been asleep for," she checked her watch, "twenty-eight hours? Since you got home, anyway."

Jeff slumped back in the chair, confused. Sal came out with his drink, perching it on the wide arm of his chair.

"I've got to go into work, hon. Will you be okay 'til I get back?"

"He'll be fine, darling, I'm here all day."

Sal looked at Jeff until he nodded his consent, then left, still looking unsure.

"She's worried."

"I know."

"We're all worried."

"Well, you can include me in that list too. It's not like I'm taking this lightly."

"Okay, okay, don't snap at me."

"I'm sorry, Anya." Jeff reached out a conciliatory hand. "I know you're all worried, and I appreciate it. Genuinely. But I'm trying to find a way to solve this, I am. I don't want this to carry on any more than you do." He pulled the notebook out of the pocket of his dressing gown.

"What's that?"

"My notes. Everything I can remember about the visions. Trying to see if I can find some kind of clue, anything that might help me understand what's going on."

"And?"

Jeff flicked through the pages. "He, Jezz, me, I guess. Well, he thinks I'm the psychosis."

"What? What do you mean?"

"When I'm him, his life feels as real to him as mine does to me. He sees me as a psychotic vision exactly the same way I see him."

"So what are you saying?"

Jeff leaned forward and rubbed at his eyes. "I don't know. It's crazy. Two lives, two personas, both the reality as far as they're concerned. I mean, I know this..." He gestured at the garden and house around them, "I *know* this is real. But he's just as sure that he is. I mean, I guess I know this is real..."

Anya reached out to him. "Be careful, darling. Don't let your mind go down that route. Of course this is real. You know what Doctor Singh said, this might seem crazy, but your symptoms are not unique to you. You're suffering psychoses, and when they find the right medication for you, they can stop it."

"I know, I know. But I keep thinking. What if...?"

"Darling, please... don't do this to yourself."

"But hear me out. I need to say this out loud."

Anya, her eyes brimming, held her hand to her mouth and nodded.

"His visions, if that's they are, make sense. He's in a war, a desperate war against an invading army that could shatter his world. Doesn't it make sense that his mind would try and create a safe place to retreat to? A safe place like this? But why am I... why would my mind need to create... that?"

Anya couldn't answer for a moment, as tears dropped down from her eyes over the hand still clamped to her mouth. Then she took a deep breath and brushed the tears away. "You've been so unhappy, darling, for so long. I don't think you've been truly happy since your mother passed away. You hate your job, you live alone, and until Sal came along you've *been* alone. You've no other purpose. Maybe your mind is just creating somewhere where you feel needed, somewhere you have purpose, responsibility. Your life, darling," and here she sobbed a little, "Your life is directionless, empty. We've tried so hard to be a family for you, but you've never truly accepted that, not really."

Jeff's eyes were streaming too by now. He held out his hand and Anya grabbed it, tightly.

"With a life that, to you, seems so empty, maybe your mind is just trying to create somewhere where you think you matter. But, darling, you do matter. You matter here, to us. I may have tried to be a mother to you when you were young because of my love for Jack, and maybe that's still part of it, but I'm trying to be a mother to you now because I love *you*. Anoushka loves you. Darling, it's tearing us up inside to watch you go through this. Not least of all because you seem to go through it all believing it's just yours to bear. But we bear it too, my love."

Jeff sobbed. "I'm sorry…"

"Hush, darling, you have nothing to apologise for. But we just want you to open up to us, to open up that last door to your heart and accept that we are your family. And maybe that will give you the strength to deal with this, give your life the colour and richness it needs, that you deserve. You're not alone, darling. You're not alone."

Jeff lay on the sofa in Jack's study, the open copy of Maugham on the floor beside him, studying the pages of his notebook. On the last page of which were drawn two bubbles, arrows going from each to the other. In one, was written 'Jeff imagines a world in which he has purpose'. In the other, 'Jezz imagines a world in which he has safety'. In a third bubble, 'The Pale woman?' He dropped the notebook on the floor and stared up at the ceiling.

He remembered, vividly now, Jezz's decision to wrap things up, to come here, say his goodbyes and go back, finally, permanently, to stand by his friends and face up to his responsibilities.

But he wasn't Jezz. He was Jeff. And his responsibilities were here, to Anya and to Anoush. To Sal. His family needed him as much as he now realised he needed them. And deep down he knew he had no doubts. They *were* real, he'd grown up with them. He had resented Anya, as strongly as he now loved her, for much of his life. That wasn't some construct, that was who he was. The ungrateful, spoilt child of a widower who had just tried to restore a little happiness to his life, and that of his son. Jeff looked up at the picture of Jack and Melissa. "I'm sorry, Dad," he whispered. "I left it too late for you to see me love them. But I do, I always did."

He wiped at his eyes, sore now from all the crying.

But inside, somewhere buried deep, he couldn't shake the last little bit of Jezz that was still there. That minuscule shadow of doubt that kept reminding him of Price, and Teemu.

"Dammit, this is ridiculous."

He got up from the couch and left the study.

A few streets away from Anya's house, down the hill, there was a section of old city wall still standing, crumbling, by the river. There was a bench there, one that Jeff had spent many an hour of his youth sat on, drinking. Sometimes with buddies and sometimes alone, when he didn't want to go home and face his father playing happy families with 'that woman'.

Jeff sat there now, watching the river as it flowed into town. At his feet, a small pile of cigarette butts was accumulating, and he lit another one now. He was cold, and uncomfortable, the bench having no back and therefore offering no support to his tired and aching torso. But still he sat, looking into the water and trying to make sense of everything going on, trying to ignore the acrid, oily smell in his nostrils.

"It's not easy, is it."

The pale woman sat next to him, the hood of her coat pulled firmly forward so from the side, all Jeff could see was platinum blonde hair sticking out from it.

"You won't tell me, I take it."

"Tell you what?"

"What's happening, what's real. What I should do."

"How can I? I don't have any answers. This dichotomy is my cross to bear as much as it is yours. If not more so."

"What the hell does that mean? Who are you in this, where do you fit in?"

"I think… I think if we knew that…" The pale woman coughed, almost choking it seemed, and put her head between her knees as she brought up a mouthful of dark, oily phlegm.

"Are you okay?" he found himself asking.

After a moment, she sat up again, wiping her sleeve across her mouth. "It's getting worse, Jeff. We don't have much time."

Jeff ground his cigarette beneath his trainer.

"This is bullshit," he said, exhaling a plume of smoke.

"But it's our bullshit."

"Awesome."

"So, what happens now? Are we looking for purpose? For safety? For family? What's keeping us here? What are we afraid of finding out?"

He didn't look at her but kept his eyes on the river.

He made a decision.

11

Station 86 floated high above the planet, tracing the same orbit it had for decades, ever in pursuit of Station 87, ever pursued by Station 84, its huge solar panels like dragonfly wings. From 86's perspective, a fiery ribbon of light was just forming around the Earth's outer edge; the sun, rising. In his office, Doctor Soong stood by the view panel, currently showing the external view down onto the planet's surface. The view panel was a luxury afforded him by his status. For most of those on the station who were still awake, the only opportunity to gaze down at their former home was in the public gallery. For the majority, however, there was no view, just an endless sleep cycle.

As the sun rose and illuminated the Earth, Soong stared down at the white planet. His heart ached with the loss of his ancestral home, yet at the same time it sung with the deathless beauty of the icebound globe. To think, his people, his grandparents, had once stridden the surface, masters of all they surveyed. The thought never failed to bring a lump to his throat. Silly old fool, he thought to himself. Getting sentimental in your old age. Soong's hair was as white as the planet, only his white veil revealed far more of the pitted, craggy surface beneath.

The door to his office opened. His assistant, with the daily reports. Soong turned and smiled at her.

"Good morning, Estelle."

"Doctor Soong," she replied. Though her features were pinched, sharp, almost severe, the smile she gave him in return was warm and affectionate. Her eyes, however, betrayed her concern. "You've not been to bed." It wasn't a question.

Soong held his hands up. "I admit it! Report me!" He chuckled, his laughter the warm sound of old leather.

"We can't have you getting ill, Doctor Soong. You need to take care of yourself." She placed a small sheaf of papers on his desk, along with the doctor's morning cup of coffee. The full details of the reports were, of course, easily accessible via his desktop interface but Soong preferred the headlines in a form that didn't require him to stare at a screen. His eyes were not what they were, and lately he found the interface display was starting to give him headaches.

Estelle sat in the chair the other side of the desk and took out her tablet, flicking through a series of programmes as she waited for her boss to drink his coffee and assimilate the briefing she had prepared. There would then be the usual discussion about priorities for the day, before she left him to his work.

Soong took his seat, picked up the report and sipped at his coffee as he started to read.

"Still no communication from the Titan colony," he noted, mournfully.

Estelle looked up briefly. "I'm afraid not. There's a rescue mission being prepared from Europa, but I'm afraid nobody's expecting them to find anyone still alive.

"Iapetus all over again," murmured Soong.

"Looks like," replied Estelle.

"Oh, my dear, I'm sorry, I wasn't thinking."

Estelle waved a hand and gave the doctor a wan smile. Her brother's family had all perished on Iapetus, but she had learned to bury the pain that came with any reference to the failed colony attempt. So much pain, shared by so many people. It seemed selfish to dwell too much on one's own.

"The Martian situation appears to be improving," she said, changing the subject.

"Hmm? Oh, yes," said Soong, flipping through the stapled sheets and finding the relevant section. "Food production stabilised, worker grievances finally being discussed by all parties. That is good news." Good news hardly began to describe it. Mars was by far the largest supplier of food in the solar system and the threat of political upheaval posed by the worker insurrection had taken humanity closer to the brink than it had been since the exodus. As it was, work on increasing their hibernation capacity had been escalated dramatically on all the remaining Earth stations, in readiness for a return to stasis, should it be necessary.

That led Soong to turn to the pertinent section. "We're still behind on module renovation, I see." He frowned.

"You've a meeting today with Levy's section. He's still arguing strongly for waiting until his work on the v6 to be completed, rather than committing to the v5."

"Yet meanwhile, our potential capacity is at 50% of most of the other stations, and that all in v4 units."

"Levy considers the v6 to be a vast improvement on the v5, and so worth the wait." Estelle put her tablet down and looked straight at Soong. "I don't care for Levy any more than you do, Doctor. He's brusque, to the point of rudeness, and notoriously difficult to negotiate with. But he knows hibernation. If you look at his full report, he makes a compelling case. In-hib stress levels in his v6 test units are way, way down. His progress in that direction represents a huge leap forward, and now that we've isolated the issues with fluid turnover, occupant stress levels are the single highest cause of early emergence."

"Yes, yes. I know, if we can keep occupants dormant, we can keep them in stasis longer..."

"Far longer," continued Estelle. "He's predicting a drop in early emergence of anything up to 80% in the v6."

"Eighty per cent?" Soong looked startled.

Estelle nodded.

"Okay, can you tag his report? I'll make sure I read it thoroughly before I meet him. Anything else?"

"Nothing that can't wait," said Estelle. She tapped a couple of icons on her tablet, then put it down again. "We've a visit from the Inspectorate due this evening."

"That seems to come around sooner every time."

Estelle shrugged. "The fewer stations, the less time it takes."

"Quite," said Soong, sadly. "Will Doctor Alterman be coming over with them, do you know?"

Estelle smiled. "I'm sure Grace wouldn't miss the opportunity to see us, Doctor Soong."

Soong cleared his throat. "That will be all, thank you, Estelle."

"You know as well as I do, Wendall, that the stress levels of occupants in hibernation is the biggest factor in early emergence. If we can achieve a significant reduction in stress, and I absolutely believe with the v6 we can, then we can reduce early emergence by over 70%."

"Your report said 80%, Matthew."

Levy rubbed at his moustache. "Possibly yes. Well, probably. But you know I don't like to over promise, Wendall."

Doctor Soong turned his attention again to the projection on the meeting room wall. Levy stared at him as he did so. There were only two other people present in the meeting, both Levy's assistants, the slight Chinese woman and the large, bearded European making a strikingly mismatched pair. Soong, as he usually did, had attended alone. Other people gathered assistants around them to appear important; Soong did the complete opposite, for the same reason.

Levy leaned forward. "I know I can be a prick, Wendall, I'm well aware of my own failings. But I urge you to listen to me on this one. The v6 is a huge leap forward in hibernation tech. If we get this right, we can render the whole stasis situation not only more sustainable, but also a lot less traumatic for the individual. Do you have any idea how low re-occupancy levels are amongst early emergers? Most won't go back in; they say the nightmares are all but intolerable. If you let me delay implementing the capacity increase for just a few months until the v6 is ready, I will give you a system that will have immeasurable long-term benefits."

Soong was silent for a short while. Then he came to a decision. "You're right, Matthew, you can be a prick." Levy started to roll his eyes but Soong waved a hand. "But you know your business. You're confident of the figures here?"

"I'd stake my reputation on it."

"Good. You just did. I can give you three months, then I need something concrete to show the Inspectorate. Until then, I'll keep them off your back."

Levy sighed and leant back in his chair. "Thanks, Wendall. We won't let you down."

Doctor Soong smiled his gentle smile. "I should let you get on." He stood up. There was nothing on the table for him to collect, no tablet, no drink. As well as attending meetings with no assistants, Soong made a point of doing so empty handed. It was up to other people to provide the data and the reports, Soong's only job was to make decisions, and for that all he needed was his mind. He shook Levy's hand, then left the meeting room.

One of Levy's assistants, Eleanor, tossed her stylus on to the table, rolling her eyes as she stretched out. "Jeez, I though the ancient old bastard was never going to say yes." The other, an overweight bearded man called Victor, chuckled in response.

"That old bastard," growled Levy through his moustache, "was running this station when he was only a few years older than you are, and when you're his age, you two will still be my fucking assistants. Get to work."

"Yes boss," replied Eleanor, chastened.

Soong sat in his quarters, drinking a glass of wine and largely ignoring the plate of soy noodles in front of him. Instead, he was gazing fondly at Grace Alterman, his opposite number on Station 87. She, in return, was giving him a wry smile.

"I'm not sure the Inspectorate would take too kindly to that, Wendall."

"Come on, it's not like there's actual rules against it." Grace was aging well, he thought. The lines in her face spoke of the stress of managing an orbital facility in a decaying system, and she was stick-thin, but her massive, wild shock of curls, tied back in a workaday fashion, still contained but a few grey hairs. There was also an indefatigable air of *life* about her.

She took a sip of wine, then put her glass down. "No, true. But we both know they wouldn't like it, two adjacent station directors fraternising… I don't want to get posted to another station or, God forbid, recalled. It's just for one visit. Next time, I promise."

Soong sighed. "You're probably right. It's just that I miss you, Grace. I barely sleep any more, I find it so much easier when you're in the bed with me."

"Thanks!"

They both laughed.

"You know what I mean. It's a comfort. I'm not saying I want to sleep all the time…" He gave her a wink, and she raised a hand, still holding chopsticks, to cover her mouth in an endearing display of modesty.

"You're incorrigible, you old rogue."

"Hey, at our age, it's charming."

"At *your* age, it oughtn't to be allowed."

Soong feigned a frown. "I should be wounded by that."

Grace smiled playfully. "Somehow, I think you'll survive."

A low buzz sounded from a console by the door.

"Excuse me," said Soong.

"I'll be waiting," replied Grace, playfully.

He was still smiling as he stood and walked over to the console, but when he arrived by it and read the notification, he frowned.

Grace, turning in her chair to watch him, saw the change in his demeanour. "Problem?"

"Early emergence. Our third this cycle. This one's been coming a while. I should get down there."

"Do you need to be present? It's a bit below your paygrade, Director." Grace was more puzzled than anything. The disruption to their meal was frustrating, but there were always other meals.

"This case is, umm, more complicated. Besides, I'm still a qualified physician. I like to keep my skills fresh."

Grace had stood, and was now beside him at the console, reading the notification over his shoulder.

"Is that…?"

Soong took a deep breath. "Yes. Elaine's partner. They, ah, don't know yet. About Iapetus. I want to be there to break it to them."

Grace put a hand up and gently laid it on Soong's arm, where he covered it with his own. He patted her hand, then reached out for the door panel.

"Would you like me to come with you?" she asked.

"I think not, my dear. Perhaps you'd better be getting back."

Doctor Soong made his way through the station to the long-term hibernation facility. He was met along the way by Levy, Eleanor and Victor in tow. "I wasn't expecting to see you, Matthew. Do you attend every emergence?"

Levy looked briefly uncomfortable. "No, I, ah, knew you'd be attending, Wendall. I just, well..."

Soong glanced over at his Head of Hibernetics, trying not to make the surprise too visible. "Thank you," he said, softly.

Levy cleared his throat as he checked the report on his tablet. "We're definitely too far gone for resettlement. Occupant's heartrate and brain activity have passed tipping point. At this point, waking is our only option."

"I understand." The group reached the door to the hibernation facility. "Well, then. Shall we?"

Inside, they were met by Doctor Anwen, the facility administrator, a young woman with short, cropped, artificially blonde hair. Kind eyes, Soong always thought, an enchanting green...

"Doctor Soong, I'm sorry to have disturbed you, but I..."

Soong waved away her apologies. "You did the right thing, Alice. I should be here for this."

Anwen nodded, then turned and led the group through the administration office and into the changing rooms where they all reached for, and started to pull on, the required sterility suits. None of them needed reminding of the protocols but nevertheless, they were supervised by one of Doctor Anwen's assistants, a thin, freckled woman with straggly red hair, who checked the fastenings on their sterility suits, checking items off on her handheld tablet as she did so.

Gloved, booted, suited and helmeted, the 'LTH' logo prominently displayed on all the gear, the five of them then stepped through into the decontamination chamber, Victor bringing with him a gurney and Eleanor carrying a medikit. They were blasted with a quick biowash, then finally, they went through to the long-term hibernation storage.

Soong all but gasped as he took in the chamber. It didn't seem to matter how many times he came in here, the significance of the facility never failed to hit home when you actually saw it. The dimensions wouldn't have been considered impressive on a surface facility, but for a space station, the room was enormous. Row upon row of black, lozenge-shaped pods were arrayed on multiple levels. There were six hundred pods in this chamber, one of ten that formed the vast majority of Station 86's structure, itself one of five hundred such stations orbiting the planet. More stations of this kind orbited every other planet and planetary-mass moon in the solar system it had been possible to float them around. Millions upon millions of human souls held in stasis, the fraction of humanity it had been possible to save.

The party made their way along the walkway between the pods, Anwen checking each display as they passed. Approximately a third of the way down the row, she stopped, indicating the pod they were looking for. Even had he not known what he was looking at, the colour of the text on the display, and the rapidly changing numbers, would have told Soong that something was happening in this pod that was not happening in the dozens they had passed to get to this point.

Anwen checked something on her commlink to the control room, then turned to Soong. "Doctor Soong, it'll be another couple of minutes before the emergence window is reached. I'm sorry, my timing was a little off."

"It's fine, Doctor Anwen. I know how complicated a science it is. We all do, eh, Doctor Levy?"

Anyone looking through Levy's facemask at that point would have assumed that being asked to wait for two minutes was some kind of insult to his culture, but he coughed and gave a brief assertion of agreement.

As Anwen took advantage of the opportunity to visually inspect more of the surrounding pods, Soong tentatively reached out a hand to touch the pod with the unsettled occupant. Through the sterility suit, his sense of touch was limited, beyond detecting the basic solidity of the object. The temperature was necessarily as low as possible within the chamber anyway, so it came as no surprise that it felt cold to the touch. Slippery, too, with water condensing on the surface. There was no seeing into the pod, no convenient glass panel to show the face of the person within. Maintaining the integrity of the pod and stabilising the conditions within had proven hard enough without the incorporation of an unnecessary component such as a viewing plate. A solitary pipe connected the pod to the supply of the necessary formulation that could keep the human body in good health during stasis. That and a surprisingly small number of biosensors were the only connection between the outside world and the halted life within. The pod itself resembled nothing more than some kind of alien egg, Soong always thought. Quite honestly, they gave him the willies.

At a touch on his arm, Soong started and, crouching as he was, nearly fell over. He allowed Anwen to help him back to a standing position. "Squatting, you know. Not so easy at my age."

"We're ready to begin the emergence, Doctor Soong."

"Very well, let's press on."

The complexities of the emergence procedure, Soong was familiar with, to an extent. But Anwen and Levy ran the initial operation, with backup from the control room, who had a more extensive relay of information from the pod sensors than Anwen had on the small panel in the chamber.

She slowly brought the pod's temperature up, adjusting the mix of the formulation being circulated through the pod. Brain activity readings and heartrate increased further as she did so, and before long, she looked up at Levy and gave him the nod. He and Victor lowered the pod onto the chamber floor, with Eleanor standing to the rear, ensuring the supply pipe stayed connected and didn't kink.

The pod, until this point to all appearances a single, seamless structure, gave off a hiss, and a crack in the shell appeared, running around the entire perimeter. A thick, viscous liquid like honey oozed out of the gap. Even through the sterility suits, the acrid, oily smell was almost choking, making Soong gag as he took an involuntary step backwards. More of the liquid was escaping the pod now, running down through the grated walkway. The drainage canal beneath collected the liquid and conveyed it back to the tanks where it was treated, recycled, and pumped back into the supply that fed every pod on the station. Then, as Levy and Victor lifted the lid of the pod, a wave of fluid poured out like a tsunami-in-miniature, essentially halving its capacity for retaining the liquid.

Soong couldn't stop himself from craning his neck around the form of Levy to see into the pod as soon as the lid was removed. He hadn't seen the occupant for coming up to two decades and, as nervous as he was, his curiosity was stronger. To see someone who hadn't aged at all whilst he had grown twenty years older and frailer, it still captured his active imagination. The technological miracle of it!

Curled up in the foetal position, the occupant was, so far as could be determined under the thick gloop that still covered them, deathly pale. Without natural exposure to the sun, of course, they all were, but hibernation exacerbated it and the figure looked as if made of porcelain. Slowly, uncomfortably, Soong got down on his knees and went as if to reach a hand out and touch the figure, though he could not bring himself to actually do so.

Anwen leant down beside him. "It will still take a moment, Doctor Soong." She looked up at Eleanor, who had now taken Anwen's place at the console and was monitoring the sensor feeds. Levy's assistant nodded. There were no apparent immediate issues.

"Of course," replied Soong, softly.

Anwen turned to Levy and, at her signal, he reached into the pod, his distaste at coming into contact with the gloop transparent, and placed a small device on the figure's chest. Bringing the occupant's heart rate up to normal levels, he dropped the device and made a grab for them as they started to cough, choking on the honey-like liquid that had, until this point, been keeping them alive. Victor reached down as well, and between him and Levy, they pulled the occupant's torso up and over the side of the pod, the action tilting the pod up so more of the liquid flowed out into the drainage gulley. Levy pulled another device from the medikit and wrestled it into the occupant's mouth with his fingers, forcing in a liquid that would, harmlessly, react with the honey-like fluid and reduce its viscosity. Moving ever-more freely now, the liquid trickled, then poured out of the occupant's mouth as they vomited. The vomit was thick and dark in colour, and it dripped down through the walkway into the gulley. It would be harmlessly extracted from the formula in the processing tanks.

Coughing now, the occupant put out their hands as if to push themselves up, but the atrophying of their muscles made the attempt a vain one. Levy tactfully made way for Soong beside the figure.

"You're okay, don't panic. You've just come out of long-term hibernation," said Soong smoothly, his arm around the figure. As the coughing desisted, he turned the occupant around until they lay nestled in his lap. Wiping at the gloop, trying to clean the occupant's face, he looked down on the figure tenderly. "You'll feel pretty terrible for a while," he smiled, kindly. "But this will pass. You're back with us now. Can you hear me? Do you understand what I'm saying?"

The pale woman's eyes opened, blinking rapidly and darting all over the place. She groaned.

"It's okay. It's Doctor Soong, I'm here," he cooed, softly. "Jess, I'm here. Can you hear me, Jess? You're okay. You're okay, Jess."

ACKNOWLEDGEMENTS

Thank you to Henry, for starting me out on this road, and to Angel, for picking up the baton and running with it.

Thank you to my wife, and to Mum & Dad, Rob and Steve for the unconditional love and support.

Thank you to God for, I suppose, pretty much everything.

Thank you to you, you absolute legend, for reading this.

www.ingramcontent.com/pod-product-compliance
Lightning Source LLC
Chambersburg PA
CBHW032002180726

48283CB00008B/2529